4 out of 5 stars as rated by readers at OnlineBookClub.org

DEATH

— IS THE —

LIMIT

RISE AND RISE UNTIL YOU CANT ANYMORE,
ONLY DEATH CAN STOP YOU BABY.

KGAOGELO AGGREY MOKONE

First Published 2023 by Kgaogelo Aggrey Mokone
Copyright © 2023 Kgaogelo Aggrey Mokone

ISBN 978-0-7961-3386-1 (Print)

Cover and interior crafted with love by the team at
www.myebook.online

CONTENTS

1. Where dreams begin   1
2. The high school days   13
3. Becoming 'Sky'   23
4. Welcome and romance   33
5. Music at Mzala   43
6. Singing for the college   56
7. Sky's rise   73
8. The recording artist   83
9. The wealthy music star   100
10. Grieving nation   121

About the Author   143

CHAPTER 1
WHERE DREAMS BEGIN

I t's a small village with big dreams. Makometsane village is situated in Mpumalanga to the west of the border with Limpopo, and about a hundred and twenty kilometres north of Emalahleni and the N4 as the crow flies. The nineties in 'Mak ville', as they called it, was a time when television was starting to dominate every home. It was a decade of music – and the youth yearned to become musicians, to appear on television or FM radio like the famous musicians they listened to.

In the homes there was either a one-speaker FM radio using batteries, or the four-step music system. For boys it was swag to have a car radio in their bedroom with car speakers – and because they could not play the radio with a car battery, big Nokia phone chargers were used to connect to the radio. Then the radio could be connected to the car speakers built into a box to give more sound. Sometimes amplifiers were added to boost the speakers.

Mak ville was interesting and beautiful with the Moutse

Nature Reserve to the south and the big Moutse Dam and the Moutse River rushing from south to north. Mak ville was so small you could hear the river flow during the rainy season at night. The town of Siyabuswa is about twenty kilometres to the west of Mak ville, Waterval and Maphotla are to the south, Allemansdrift is to the east, and Senotlelo is to the north. The R568 road goes through the middle of the village from Pretoria to Limpopo. The roads were gravel and you could hear a bus coming from a distance, with dust appearing before the bus reached the village.

Mak ville is situated in tribal land, headed by a Chief, and when a matter concerning the community arose, a piece of steel would be hit with a hammer, making a sound that carried through the whole community, calling them to gather for a meeting, a *lekgotla*. They knew each other and if you were not from the village you would quickly be recognised.

Driving from the east to west on the R568, at the end of the village on the right hand side was a white house with big yard and a fence that was falling down in some places because of rotten poles holding it. It was the home of the Molapo family, an average family just like any other in the village. The community respected the family because they were first responders in every community matter, good or bad. Even the Chief would appoint Mr Molapo in some of the community work to supervise. Sefako Molapo was a community welder – this was a skill that he learnt from his father – he was not educated, but he knew how to read and write.

He made a living building things with steel, or fixing

things using two-bottle gas and a welding machine. He sometimes built burglar bars, but they were not that common as crime was not bad in the area.

Sefako charmed Mrs Baby Molapo, which was not surprising as he was a charming, coffee-coloured, tall and muscular man. Baby would melt when she saw him returning home from wherever he had been working – and she never tired of being near her husband. She was a good match for Sefako; light in colour, well built from top to bottom and front to back, a short woman with strong legs; an African woman indeed, blessed at the back with beautiful curves. Baby had a small pointy nose, brown eyes, small pink lips, and a beautiful smile showing white teeth with a gap.

Sefako and Baby would sometimes walk to Moutse River, to the bridge that crosses to Senotlelo, walking slowly and romantically as Sefako whispered sweet nothings in Baby's ear and Baby walked as if she did not want to look shy. The two were so in love that if we heard stories that a man was trying to seduce Baby or a woman was trying to seduce Sefako we would know it was not true because they were always together. Even though Baby was not educated, she was naturally intelligent – and both she and Sefako loved to learn. She planted an orchard of mango trees and sold the fruit on the R568 when it was in season.

Sefako appreciated that his wife was always there when situations got tough. Sefako was a quiet person and Baby was talkative, but they were both down-to-earth and doted on each other, and they had respect for the Mak ville community. Mak ville was a good place to raise a family.

Sefako and other men would go fishing on weekends as another way of feeding their families and source of income.

In the summer of 1975, on 1 December, Sefako and Baby were blessed with a baby girl, who they named Lucky. Everyone in the community came to see the little baby and bring gifts for her. She grew to be a cute little girl with a small pointy nose, brown eyes, and small pink lips, just like her mother.

After the birth of Lucky, doctors told Sefako and Baby that she could not have another child because she no longer had productive eggs. There were difficulties when Lucky was born and there was a chance that little Lucky would not survive, but through God's grace she survived – and the doctors said it was a miracle. That's why she was given the name Lucky. Her full name was Lucky Atlega Molapo. Sefako and Baby raised Lucky well, she was not spoilt, but she was given all she needed. Lucky grew up in a community that loved her, and as a disciplined child, she helped anyone who needed help. Her friends gave her the nickname KP, '*Kgopela Lucky,*' which means 'ask Lucky'.

She was a good-looking talkative girl with good manners, and she was active. She loved to play with other kids, always sharing because that was what she was taught at home. At the age of five, Lucky attended school at Moutse Primary School with other village friends. On Lucky's first day at school, Baby left her with the other children and Teacher Mmabatho Modise, but her heart was broken about leaving little Lucky with strangers. As she slowly walked away, she looked back and saw that little Lucky was happy. She was talking to Teacher Mmabatho as if she had been going to school for a long time. Baby walked on with tears falling down her cheeks. She was happy that her only child was going to school for the first time, and proud to be the mother of a happy child. Wherever she went with Lucky, people showed love for little Lucky; she was a miracle from above.

Lucky was a good girl at school; she was bright in class and she produced good results. When Teacher Mmabatho needed something, she would send Lucky. Lucky had a voice that was louder than the other children's when they were singing or talking. All the teachers were amazed by Lucky's behaviour; she showed such respect for a child of her age. Lucky also mixed happily with both boys and girls, and at lunchtime she would be singing and running around with friends, or just sitting and playing with books, drawing and colouring.

After school, Lucky went home with her friend Lebogang, who was not only a friend, but a neighbour as well. They grew up playing together as Lebo lived only a few steps away from Lucky's home. Lebo was the last born to her parents, Mr and Mrs Monkoe. Her two older brothers, Thabo and Thabang, were always busy with their own business and didn't pay any attention to Lebo, so Lebo regarded Lucky as a sister, not only a friend. Lucky was happy to have Lebo as a friend because it meant she always had someone to play with.

One hot summer's day at school, during a free period, Principal Noko came out of his office and walked to the standard five class in block B, which was Lucky's class. Her desk was positioned in front of the classroom so that a person entering would be face-to-face with Lucky. She was sitting with Lebo, chatting about the past weekend when she had helped her mother sell fruit on the R568. Sometimes Lucky went with her mother to sell mangos under a tree on the R568 on weekends – she would watch her mother talk to strangers who stopped to buy, or she would help to sell mangos, but also play with a doll that her mother had made for her. Lucky was happy to see white people passing on their way to Moutse Dam to fish. It was rare to see white people at Mak ville, and it was a surprising experience for little Lucky. When a vehicle approached, they could see it coming from far off, and when it approached, the billowing dust would make it hard to see who the driver was. Was it a white men going to fish? Would the vehicle stop and buy? Or where was it going? Lucky was a curious child.

Anyway, the class was making a noise, talking about things that did not involve school lessons when Principal Noko appeared at the door. Suddenly the class was silent and Principal Noko started calling out the names of the children he saw talking. In those days corporal punishment was still a reality, and Lucky and Lebo were among the noisemakers as usual; Principal Noko heard Lucky's voice because it was loud. Principal Noko's punishment often entailed two whips on their buttocks, but that day he was in a good mood – and anyway he was not that cruel – so he gave them a choice of punishment, to either run eight hundred metres on the football ground or clean the block B classes.

But to Lucky he said, "Lucky, I heard your voice from the office. You are going to sing in the school choir and for the rest of the semester you will give us a song at assembly every day." The punishment was hard and easy at the same time; it was easy for Lucky to sing in the school choir, but hard to sing at assembly. None of the children wanted to sing at assembly in front of the whole school, but thanks to noisemaker Lucky, she saved the rest of the school from that fate. She had to join the choir with immediate effect, and that afternoon she went to the school hall … there stood Teacher Moloko Makgoba. Mrs Makgoba was a big, ugly woman with red eyes, who never had a smile or a friendly face; she was a giant with a good singing voice.

Teacher Makgoba was a member of the community choir and she was a lead singer at the church she attended. She started singing in her high school choir, and they say that in her school days at Mokebe High School, she was the lead singer in the choir and the school won many competitions and collected many awards. Singing was a hobby for Teacher Makgoba, and music followed her to Moutse Primary School where Principal Noko asked her to be the choir teacher.

Lucky greeted her, "Afternoon Teacher Principal …" Before she could finish, Teacher Makgoba responded, "I knew you were coming. Sing me a gospel song you know." She decided to sing a well-known song from those days, '*Jerusalem ikhaya lami.*' Lucky took a deep breath because she was scared, she settled her voice and then started singing, looking at the teachers and also turning to the choir, with her hand on her chest. Lucky's voice was so amazing it was as if she was highly experienced, but in fact she didn't sing, not even at assembly. When other children sang, she just moved her lips. The choir was amazed and shocked at the same time because they did not know that she had a velvet voice.

Principal Noko was passing the hall door; he stopped, smiled, and when she finished singing, he walked away with a big smile on his face, shaking his head, and saying to himself, "She is the one." Teacher Makgoba shed tears; she was reminded of the time when she was a lead singer. She pointed to her first row where the lead singers were standing. They opened a space for Lucky, smiling, and from that day, she became a singer in the school choir. Teacher Makgoba had been looking for a lead singer, and Lucky was the best of the best; indeed she was the one. The choir was surprised to see Teacher Makgoba smiling because she never smiled at anyone, and from then on she looked happy every day. The question was whether her expression changed because of Lucky's voice or because she found the lead singer she had been looking for so long.

The next day Lucky did what Principal Noko had instructed and sang a song at assembly. She went to the front on the 'stoep' where the teachers and principal were standing and took a deep breath. She fixed her voice and sang an assembly gospel song, with learners following and providing back up singing. The teachers were surprised how high the singing spirit was that day. Teachers sang together with the kids, whose hands were waving above their heads, and even those who never sang at assembly were singing. In the middle of the song, Lucky stopped the song and immediately started a new song with her velvet voice and a lot of energy. Wow! Teachers were surprised at the dancing and praising the Lord as if they were in church. Lucky continued for about fifteen minutes without a break, and even the teachers forgot that assembly time has passed.

After assembly, learners went to class and teachers to the staff room to prepare for classes, and Lucky and her velvety voice was the topic of conversation in the staff room. Lucky sang as if she was an adult and her teachers thought she was born to be a singer, but that Lucky was not aware of the talent yet. Lucky continued to sing every day at assembly and in the afternoons, she attended choir practice.

Teacher Makgoba was happy with how well Lucky did in the choir as lead singer, and she trained her to write new songs for the choir. The lead backup singer was Sinko Kola, a boy with a positive attitude who was dedicated in everything he did. He was a short, slender and charming boy with a thick voice; he loved singing, especially when Lucky was leading, and he loved the songs that Lucky wrote for the choir. Lucky also loved to write songs that needed a lead backup singer.

Sefako and Baby heard that their daughter was a good singer and songwriter at school, and they were proud, especially when teachers told them that she was bright in class. "Lucky is writing choir songs?" they asked themselves. Many others also asked that question because Lucky was only in standard five. Lucky's parents were proud, but not excited; their only focus for Lucky was to get a good education, and they did not care much about her talent.

Two weeks before the choir competition, in which the first prize winners were going to receive gold medals and a cup for the school, the choir started to practice every day to prepare for the competition. Principal Noko also gave them an extra hour to do their homework before practice. In those two weeks, Lucky would arrive home tired. Her mother noticed, and gave her a break from doing household chores so she could rest. Lucky would drop her school bag on her bed, eat, bath, and then sleep. That was her daily routine for two weeks and her parents were understanding. Teacher Makgoba visited their home to explain that Lucky was preparing for the school choir competition, and to invite them to come and offer their support.

The day of the school choir competition came. Lucky woke early and prepared herself for the big day. She wore her lead singer uniform, which was a white shirt, maroon skirt, long white socks, black shoes, and a maroon beret. She looked beautiful, just like her mother, with her chubby body, brown eyes, and pink lips.

Principal Noko drove them to the competition in a bakkie about thirty-six kilometres to Marapyane village at Khamani Primary School. Parents also attended the competition to support the school choir, and Sefako and Baby were among the people who were going to see the school choir sing. It was a one-day competition; visiting schools were treated well and with respect and were given rooms to rehearse in, but many of the learners were nervous because it was an unfamiliar experience.

The choirs performed one by one, until, by midday, it was announced that Moutse Primary and Khamani Primary were in the finals. Principal Noko, parents, teachers, and Teacher Makgoba were excited because this was the first time that Moutse Primary made it to the finals. They were up against the best school choir that was protecting their position of having won the school choir competition for three years in a row.

After lunch they prepared for finals. Khamani Primary was called first; it was scary because they sang so well that everyone in a hall was dancing. They sang two well-known gospel songs, before giving Moutse Primary a chance to be on stage. They walked onto the stage; Lucky was in front, followed by Sinko and the choir behind him, walking in a straight line and positioning themselves in order. Lucky started to sing. Teacher Makgoba had given the choir the chance to choose the two songs they wanted to sing, and they had chosen one song written by Lucky and one by Teacher Makgoba. Lucky started with her song, 'Glory to God.' She took a deep breath and fixed her voice as usual, and with her velvety voice she started to sing. The whole hall stood up, amazed at the beautiful singing. Baby was crying tears of joy, she could not believe how well her daughter could sing and she was proud because everyone was looking at Lucky.

> *Glory to God, the creator of heaven and earth*
> *the king of kings, master of the universe*
> *you gave me joy and happiness*
> *I am who I am because of you*

The backup lead singer came in, 'Glory … Glory' and then the choir came in behind the backup lead singer with the chorus 'Glory … Glory … Glory … to the Lord.' It continued like that for three minutes, with Lucky leading and Sinko as backup lead singer.

When they sang the second song written by Teacher

Makgoba, it was obvious that Moutse Primary were going to win. According to the judges, that one song had been enough to make a decision and they were impressed that the choir sang their own songs composed by their lead singer and their teacher. They couldn't believe that a standard five learner could write a song or sing that well, and Lucky made history that day.

CHAPTER 2
THE HIGH SCHOOL DAYS

At the end of the year, Lucky passed standard five with flying colours, and went on to high school. The nearest high school was Malebo High School. It was sad for Moutse Primary pupils because their best school choir singer was going to high school and would no longer sing for the school, but for Lucky, she was excited about the new high school experience.

It was not the end of singing for Lucky though. Malebo High had a junior and a senior choir. The junior choir was for learners from standard six to standard eight, and the senior choir for standard nine and ten – both choirs were for boys and girls.

Malebo High was five hundred metres from Moutse Primary so it was not going to be a challenge for Lucky to adjust to her new environment. The difference was that some of the learners she knew would be attending high school in other neighbouring areas. Mak ville was lucky to have both a primary school and high school that were recognised in the Mbibane region as the best schools for a quality education. Malebo High consistently achieved a ninety per cent matric pass rate every year, and it was every parent's dream to send their children to these two schools in Mak ville.

Lucky had many friends, some of whom were going to attend Malebo High, and Lebogang Monkoe was one of them. On school opening day in January 1989 at Malebo High, everyone was in class and the teachers were ready to take their classes. Just then, Mr Lentsoe Selona crossed the open space between the school blocks holding an A4 book, walking and looking at his shiny shoes while fixing his tie. Mr Selona was a clean-shaven, good-looking gentleman with a nice bright smile and pure white teeth. People would believe it if you told them he was every female teacher's crush.

He looked at Mrs Mosetsana Mokolo, smiled and said, "Hello Mrs Mokolo." She responded, "Hello Mr Selona," while looking down and blushing as she walked to her next class. Teacher Selona entered the standard six class and waved his hand, "Good morning class." The class responded, "Good morning Teacher." He introduced himself as their standard six class teacher. He then told the class that they would be voting for two class representatives, a boy and a girl, and then explained what the duties of the two 'class reps' would be.

Teacher Selona explained the voting procedure and immediately the class started to vote, whispering about the two people they going to choose. As most of the standard sixes had graduated from primary school with Lucky, it was obvious that she was their chosen female rep – indeed twenty of the twenty-five learners voted for Lucky. Bongani

Mahlangu had eighteen out of twenty-five votes and was appointed the male rep. Bongani was a quiet boy from another school in Moutse West, but he was popular from the first day in high school because he was the son of Principal Gentle Mahlangu. Principal Mahlangu was strict at school and at home. In the morning he would stand at the gate, and at exactly eight o'clock he closed the gate to latecomers. All learners who came late had to come with their parents the next day and explain why they were late. If late arrival at school continued for a month, that learner would face suspension for two weeks. Principal Mahlangu was a responsible father and principal, but he was a nightmare to the students.

After two weeks, it was time to vote for the Learners Representative Council (LRC) that would represent the learners in the problems they face at school, or changes they wanted to see. On Tuesday morning at assembly, Principal Mahlangu announced that on the next day, learners would vote for six people to be on the Learners Representative Council. The process was that all students would gather in the school hall after assembly and would then choose eight students. Those learners would be given thirty minutes to prepare a short speech to convince the learners and teachers of the changes they wanted to make at school. From those, only six would remain to be on the LRC, which was made up of a president, deputy president, secretary, deputy secretary, coordinator, and assistant coordinator.

This was the first time that Lucky and the other standard six learners had heard of LRC. She approached Teacher Selona after assembly for more information on what an LRC was and on their duties. Teacher Selona had realised that Lucky was a bright learner and could be one of the council members. He explained to the young girl politely. She was interested in being part of the LRC, and Lebo was pushing her to campaign. But it was going to be hard because there were older learners who were popular in the school, and besides that, they had never before had a standard six pupil on the council.

The previous council was experienced in fighting for the high positions of president and deputy president, but as Lucky was class representative, her class was supporting her to be on the LRC. At lunchtime, some of the former council members were campaigning to new learners to elect them onto the council. They went from group to group or to individuals sitting under trees having their lunch, asking for votes, and promising things like extra time for sports, extra lunchtime, one-hour free periods, and other things that sounded disastrous to the teachers.

Then Lucky formed a campaign team consisting of her friends, Lebo and Bongani, and other learners who supported her. Their strategy was to write messages on boxes with markers and then sing, which was a good strategy because she was indeed a great singer. Her voice was so good it attracted the attention of students who gathered around the group that was singing. The boxes were inscribed with positive messages like, *Vote for Lucky, you won't regret it. We need space to start a school garden for Agriculture students. Educational trips. Art skills to decorate our school halls,* and so on.

Lucky's voice attracted attention to the campaigning group, but learners also read the boxes that they held up high. While Lucky and others sang, Bongani and Lebo read the messages on the boxes aloud. Lucky's voice also attracted the attention of the teachers, who came out of the staff room to see what was happening. Lucky and her friends were singing and reading the messages on the boxes.

Principal Mahlangu was standing next to Teacher Selona, and with a soft voice he said, "Look after that girl, she will make history in life." Teacher Selona looked at the principal and looked back at the group. Lucky had stopped singing. She looked at the crowd, smiling, and said, "Thanks ... wait for my speech tomorrow." She was confident after her campaign that she would be part of the LRC.

The following morning after assembly, learners gathered in the school hall to vote for the Learners Representative Council as instructed. They raised their hands one by one to choose eight learners who were Jack Maloka, the former deputy president; Sonto Skosana, former secretary, and new members, Lili Baloyi, Jan Mabaso, William Manana, Nhlanhla Mtshweni, and Walter Chabalala. It was time to choose the last name. Lebogang raised her hand to choose Lucky. The election host, Teacher Mosetsana Mokolo, called out Lucky's name and learners raised their hands. Teacher Mokolo counted and then announced that the eighth name was Lucky Molapo "Go out to prepare your speeches," she told the hopeful LRC candidates.

Learners in the hall were singing while waiting for their leaders to come and give their speeches so they could vote for the top six. In the second voting, learners would write six names on a paper, fold it and put it in a box that Teacher Mokolo had at the front desk. The highest number of votes would get the position of president, going downwards, which means the least number of votes was for assistant coordinator.

The eight learners came back one by one to give their short speeches to their fellow learners who were shouting and booing, and some were clapping for the leaders they supported. After the speech, the chosen learners sat in front to wait for the results.

Teacher Mokolo counted the results and it was the decisive moment. She stood up and called out, "Quiet, quiet, quiet!" She then hit the desk with her hand. Everyone was quiet. She started reading the results, from bottom to top position. " Assistant coordinator, Lili Baloyi; coordinator Jan Mabaso; deputy secretary, William Manana; secretary, Sonto Skosana; deputy president, Jack Maloka; and finally, the president of the Learners Representative Council is Lucky Molapo!" The hall was screaming, "huu?" But the loudest voice was Lebo's who was shouting, "Lucky, Lucky, Lucky!" Bongani followed Lebogang, clapping his hands, and then suddenly everyone in a hall was shouting Lucky's name. Lucky made history again; she was the first president of the LRC in standard six, and she defeated Jack Maloka, the former president to deputy president. And it was the end of the race for Walter Chabalala and Nhlanhla Mtshweni.

It was time for the classes to resume but before that, Teacher Mokolo announced that the top six needed to gather in the hall tomorrow during the first free period for a lecture on the duties of members of the LRC.

The following day the top six gathered in the school hall, and Deputy Principal Given Mashaba and Teacher Mosetsana Mokolo lectured the council and then discussed the date of their first meeting. They decided on Wednesday the following week during the second free period. The agenda was to discuss changes needed at school, how to control late coming, complaints, and other burning issues.

Lucky continued working hard in class. She was no longer class representative because if you are on the council, you no longer qualify to be a class representative. According to school rules, she had power to choose another class rep, and she appointed Lebogang Monkoe.

LRC members were allowed to do their council work during free periods, and during the week, Lucky and other council members asked permission from Deputy Principal Mashaba and Teacher Mokolo to visit classes to ask student about changes they wanted to see at school, talk about late coming, and ask if they were interested in starting a food garden at school. The garden would also help the Agriculture learners to study practically, while also feeding underprivileged people in the community. The information would be on the agenda of the next council meeting.

It was a presentation day. President of the LRC was presenting to the council members, and Principal Mahlangu was invited to attend. Both the principal and council members were impressed; Lucky displayed a professional demeanour and she proposed initiatives such as a food garden that would develop skills, and beautify the school by using learners with art skills – she mentioned learners she knew who were good artists by name. Tommy Mamba was known in the community for his artwork that he sold on the R568 road to white people on their way to Moutse Dam. Even though Tommy was two classes ahead of Lucky, she suggested that he be given an opportunity to show his skill by painting artwork on school walls. Other learners with art skills could also come forward.

She also proposed that a black book be kept for trouble-makers and latecomers in the school. Lucky believed that the names in a black book could highlight some of the problems the school faced and be discussed with their parents in parent meetings. Lucky suggested that no learner would want their name in the black book.

Principal Mahlangu said, with a soft voice and serious face, "The suggestions are good and if there is nothing more I will give feedback soon." They discussed the date of the next meeting and agreed that Teacher Mokolo would let the council know when the principal would be available.

Weeks passed without the council getting feedback, which was sad after the hard work that they had done. The council was discouraged and they were about to give up when one day after assembly, Teacher Mokolo announced that the council must meet with Principal Mahlangu in the second free period in the school hall. The council members were happy, but they had mixed feelings.

In the meeting, Principal Mahlangu opened with prayer and reported back. He announced that the school would allocate a space for the school food garden, and would give learners with artistic skills the chance to develop their skills by introducing art at school. The school budget would include art materials, and a class would be reserved for art. However, he refused permission for the school walls to be painted with artwork by learners. He also agreed to the black book. He then dismissed the meeting. It was a win for the council and they hugged each other, laughing.

Principal Mahlangu did as he promised. The Agriculture students started the food garden, and the matric pass rate improved. Malebo High was also the first school to offer art classes in the Mbibane region. Late coming decreased too, with the black book system.

Lucky made history at Malebo High as the LRC President, and she joined the school choir as she had in primary school. At Malebo High, you normally started in the junior choir, but Lucky went straight to the senior choir because her velvety voice was recognised in assembly, and in any case, many had heard about her singing skills from primary school. It was not surprising that Lucky was the choir lead singer and the first learner at Malebo High to write choir songs, as she had at primary school.

Lucky was still president of the LRC in standard eight, and the school choir was winning competitions – she was becoming more popular at school. The only thing Lucky was not good at was sports. She tried to participate in many sporting activities at school but she was not as good as she was a singer or Council President. But she didn't give up. Netball was the sport she tried, even though her ability was lacking.

Lucky didn't fail any classes from standard six to matric – she was bright in class and excelled in all subjects. In her standard ten year, she was voted to be on the LRC, but she declined because she wanted to focus on her studies and pass with flying colours. She didn't stop singing as it helped to refresh her mind, but she didn't participate in competitions.

Lucky reduced her activities at school because her parents had saved money so she could study to be a teacher at Kwandebele College – teaching was a respected profession. Lucky wanted to pass with high marks to make them proud, but she could not quit music.

Lucky would tell her friends, *"Mmino ke bophelo baka … ke okwa gohle mo ke sepelang,"* waving her right hand slowly, rolling her eyes, and moving as if she was on a cat walk. That is Sepedi and it means, 'Music is my life and I can hear music wherever I go.' Her friends thought she was crazy; how can a person hear music everywhere if they were not crazy? Lucky was trying to express how much she loved music and that music was a part of who she was, but it was only Lebo who understood what she meant. Lucky's friends well knew that Lucky was a good singer, but they also thought she was a funny and talkative person, and they didn't take her seriously.

CHAPTER 3
BECOMING 'SKY'

Bongani Mahlangu was known to give people nicknames, and the name he gave Lucky was 'Sky'. He gave people their nicknames based on their actions, and he chose Sky for Lucky because of her big dreams – because 'the sky is the limit'. Bongani had heard his father say those words, and when his father explained the meaning to him, he realised it was the name for Lucky.

Even though her dreams sometimes sounded like fantasy, Bongani and Lebo always believed in Sky. The nickname caught on and soon everyone was calling her Sky.

Indeed Sky was wholly dedicated to everything she did. Bongani and Lebo knew that she wanted to be a singer and not a teacher, but it was in her nature to want to please her parents.

Lucky matriculated in 1993, and passed with a distinction. She was second in the school after Bongani, in the top five with Lebo, and in the top ten in the region. Malebo

High School was recognised as a disciplined school in the region with a high matric pass rate – and this year it was ninety-five per cent.

Sefako and Baby were so happy to see their daughter's name in the newspaper and they slaughtered seven big white chickens to celebrate her pass. It was a big day for Lucky and Lebo. Mr and Mrs Monkoe, their children and other neighbours came to celebrate with the Molapo family. And Principal Mahlangu, Deputy Principal Mashaba, and other teachers came to congratulate Lucky for passing with a distinction.

The Chief of Mak ville instructed his righthand man to ask at every house for a donation for Lucky to further her studies at Kwandebele College – he was proud to have one of his community's children among the top learners in the region. Lucky made her community proud; it was a small community, living in the shadow of some of the bigger surrounding communities.

Lebo's parents worked in Pretoria – her father was a gardener at a white man's house, and her mother worked in a dry cleaners. Sometimes Mr Monkoe's employers would bring him home with things they no longer needed, like beds, room dividers, kitchen units, and other items of furniture. One day they asked Lebo about her plans after matric, and just like many other kids in the area, she wanted to study at Kwandebele College. They promised to help Mr Monkoe pay for Lebo's college tuition. Her father asked her to write to Mr and Mrs Williams letting them know that she had passed matric. She did as he asked and included her matric results. The Williams were happy to receive her letter and promised to pay fifty per cent of

Lebo's tuition and her registration at the college. This was music to Lebo's ears – she was going to attend the same college as her friend Sky, doing the same course. Bongani was also going to Kwandebele College, and he was going to study Law.

Sky and Lebo were going to miss their parents, but Kwandebele College was only twenty kilometres from home and they would come home once a month, to save money. And in any case, they had each other. They had been raised closer than blood sisters and the main differ-ence between them was that Sky was a singer and Lebo was focused on a teaching career.

In January 1994, Sky and Lebo put their belongings into Principal Mahlangu's vehicle as he had volunteered to drive Sky, Lebo, and his son Bongani, to Kwandebele College for the first time. Everything was packed in the old blue Toyota bakkie that belonged to their school. They packed everything they would need for the first time at college, as well as extra things because they feared the unknown and didn't want to be stuck without things they needed. Leaving their parents for the first time was a big deal, they found.

At the front gate of the Molapo home, both Lebo's and Sky's families gathered to say goodbye to their girls, with tears of joy in their eyes. Sky and Lebo were the first members of their families to attend college and the first generation in their community to attend college.

To Bongani's family it was normal to go to college after matriculating because his father was a qualified principal and his mother was a nurse. Both had studied at Mara-pyane College, and they had met there, when Bongani's father was a second-year student and his mother was in her first year. His older brother, Thulani, was a soldier, but he had attended Marapyane College and studied Agriculture, and then chosen to serve his country. The Mahlangu family was disappointed with Thulani's decision to join the military, but they accepted that everyone must follow their own dreams.

Lebo hugged and kissed her parents goodbye, crying and happy at the same time. Sky was a strong girl; she did not cry but her face was sad. It was hard to leave her parents behind, people she had seen every day all her life.

"You are a big girl now … take care and study hard," Sefako said to her, and Baby added, "Come back home with a diploma, not a baby, … ok Lucky my baby?" Everyone laughed and Sky agreed with a nod. Mr and Mrs Monkoe also encouraged their daughter to study hard, and her brothers were proud of their little sister. It was a moment of reality when Sky, Lebo, and Bongani jumped onto the back of Principal Mahlangu's bakkie with all their belongings. The three youngsters high-fived each other at the back of the bakkie as they trundled along the dusty road, watching their families disappear in a cloud of dust.

Many members of the community were also standing along the side of the road, waving to their divas as they disappeared around the corner and left Mak ville.

The journey was long and they passed areas they had heard of but never been to. Then in the distance, they saw big buildings in the middle of nowhere. As their vehicle slowly approached the gate, they saw in big letters, 'Kwandebele College,' and they realised that this is where their journey was ending.

As they drove in, many other vehicles were also coming in, and some taxis were bringing students and dropping them at the gate. The second and third year students were busy going about their business on the campus, and many people on campus knew Principal Mahlangu because of his work in the region. He was also recognised as the person responsible for the trio who had passed matric with flying colours and were registering to attend the college. Principal Mahlangu parked the vehicle under a tree and walked in to one of the buildings. He came back a bit later and took the three into the building and into an office where a man was sitting at his desk. They greeted him, and Principal Mahlangu introduced them. "These are my kids. This is Lucky, Lebo and Bongani. These are the ones I have been up and down to register." The man introduced himself as Rector Nkadimeng, Headmaster of the College. They were all looking scared, and he said, "Don't be scared. I'm not going to bite you as long as you behave and do your work." He further explained that he had attended Marapyane College with Principal Mahlangu, and they were best friends at college. They both played soccer for the college team, called Marapyane Supers, and they joked about the 'good old days'.

While Principal Mahlangu and Rector Nkadimeng chatted about their days back in college, he asked the trio for their ID books. He was checking their ID numbers against a list on his computer, and then looked up and said, "Ok, Lucky Molepo and Lebogang Monkoe, you are going to stay in the hostel in Block A, West Wing, and Bongani Mahlangu, you are in the hostel in Block F, East Wing."

Rector Nkadimeng then went out into the corridor and

called a woman who was passing. She was Mrs Mmapule Nchabeleng, the Hostel Housekeeper. "Come inside please," he said. He then instructed Mrs Nchabeleng to take the trio to their hostels and handed her a document. "You can go with Mrs Nchabeleng. She will show you where you are going to sleep," he said. Mrs Nchabeleng greeted the trio and they responded.

Principal Mahlangu added, "I will drive to your hostels so you can offload you belongings." Principal Mahlangu was familiar with the college campus as he had often attended regional meetings there and also visited his friend, Rector Nkadimeng.

They went with Mrs Nchabeleng, passing a block that was full of queueing students, and a large building with the sign, Cafeteria, above the entrance. They also saw a sign with an arrow pointing to the swimming pool. The trio wanted to follow that arrow because they had never seen a swimming pool before; they had just heard about them, but they had to keep following Mrs Nchabeleng. They passed the soccer field, and then saw the sign to the boys hostels. They kept walking and they thought Mrs Nchabeleng might be lost, but then they saw Block F, which was where Bongani would be staying. Mrs Nchabeleng told Lucky and Lebo to wait for her, and she took Bongani to his room. It had four beds in it, but he was the only one there. Mrs Nchabeleng said, "For now you are the only one, but later three people will join you. Choose your bed and the locker opposite your bed is yours – and the keys are inside." She also told him not to trust anyone and gave him a copy of the hostel rules. She left Bongani and went back to Lucky and Lebo. "Let's go girls," she said.

They walked back the way they had come to the other side of the college and then they saw the sign 'Girls Hostel' and another sign that said, 'Block A.' They entered the hostel and went up the stairs to Room 16. Inside were two girls occupying two beds, the one nearest the door and the other second from the door. "Lerato and Popi, you have visitors," said Mrs Nchabeleng. It felt to the girls that she knew every student in the college. She introduced Lucky and Lebogang to their roommates, and then gave Lucky and Lebo their Hostel Rules and left. She came back after a few minutes to say that Principal Mahlangu was downstairs with their luggage. Before they even chose their beds, they went downstairs to collect their belongings. "Good luck. Make your parents proud," said Principal Mahlangu before saying goodbye to the girls and leaving to drop off Bongani's luggage. Principal Mahlangu was proud of the two girls and his boy, and he drove home with a big smile on his face. He first stopped at Lucky's and Lebo's homes to tell their parents that their children were safe and were settling in. "Their hostel rooms were allocated, and they will start classes very soon," he said to Sefako, Baby, and Jankie and Manana Monkoe.

Back at the women's hostel, Popi Skosana, Lerato Ranaka, Lebo Monkoe, and Lucky Atlega 'Sky' Molapo were getting along. Popi had the bed next to the door, Lerato's was second, Lebo's third, and Sky had the last bed next to the window. She was happy with her bed next to the window. She had a nice view and she could see the swimming pool, a soccer field, a netball field, and an open space next to the fence. Beyond the fence was bush that extended far into the distance.

Most of the time, the girls would sit next to the big window on Sky's bed or on chairs and gaze outside. On other days, they would sit on any of the beds to chitchat, or listen to Sky making jokes, telling long stories, or sometimes singing. Sky had special names for her friends – Popi was 'Popla', Lerato was 'Lee', and Lebogang was 'Lala'. People did not mind the names Lucky gave them – she was a crazy girl. Popi and Lerato were happy in the company of Sky and Lebo, unlike the roommates they had had in the previous semester. They told Sky and Lebo about Ginger and Mahlatse, and that Ginger was pregnant and wasn't coming back, and that Mahlatse had failed a lot and had chosen to drop out of college.

Sky with Lebo were glad to be roommates with Popi and Lerato who were second-year students and were familiar with the campus. They showed the new girls around and introduced them to other students. Sky attracted people on campus with her personality, and particularly the boys because she was beautiful.

At the boys hostel, Bongani's roommates were Jovan 'Joman' Makola, Collen 'Small' Masango, and Itumeleng Given Manaka. The boys introduced themselves to each other and immediately became friends because they were all first-year students. Joman was studying Agriculture, and Small, Itumeleng, and Bongani were all studying Law. They got along very well because they all loved education, and were able to support and advise each other when it came to serious matters.

Bongani was quiet, but he was also a mischievous boy. At home he had been quiet because his father was strict, but at college he found he had the freedom to be a boy. He talked and laughed with everyone. Itumeleng was the senior among the boys; he was a year older than the others who were all the same age. He was always the peacemaker, the intermediary, and he was a firm believer in being a team player. He believed they should take care of each other as they were all first-year students.

Joman was also talkative and a comedian. He was similar in personality to Small, who was a bit troublesome because of his small stature. The boys would pay the price of Small's wrongdoing, even if they didn't know what had been done, because, according to their rules, "Injury to one is injury to all."

On their first morning in college, Sky and her room-mates went to the Cafeteria for breakfast. After breakfast, Sky and Lebo were going to their first class, and Popla went along with them to show them their class because her classes had not yet started. Popla was studying Finance, and her classes was starting the following week. They walked out of the Cafeteria, "Bye, see you later, ladies," said Lee, going in a different direction to her Fashion Design class.

Popla, Lala and Sky continued past the library, turned right, entered a different block, and then Popla pointed out the class where Lala and Sky would be going. It was a new experience for the girls – the setup was very different to that of Malebo High; they sat on chairs at tables, unlike the desks they had in high school.

This was also the first time Lebo and Sky had seen a double-storey building; they had never visited a big city before, and to them, the campus was like a city in the middle of nowhere.

They settled in and adjusted to college life, but they

both missed their parents. Sky had a framed picture of her parents on the mirror opposite her bed, and in the mornings, she would talk to the picture before class, and then again after class. She would say "Goodbye Father and Mother!" kissing the picture in the morning, as if she was saying goodbye to them as she had every morning on her way to school. After classes, she would chat to them and tell them about her day as if they were all together. She missed them very much, but she was strong, and much of the time she tried not to think too much about home – and in any case, she knew she would be going home to visit at the end of every month.

Lala adjusted to a life of not being close to her parents and focused on her studies. She constantly reminded Sky that they must pass and make their parents proud – and be in a position to improve their families' situation at home.

Sky wanted to finish her studies and continue with her first love, her music. Lala knew Sky loved music but always advised her to focus on her studies and do her music part time. When Sky was down, Lala would tease her, saying, "Music is my life … I can feel it wherever I go," and she would do the funny actions that Sky did when she first said those words in high school. Then they would laugh together.

The girls received their books and timetable on the first day, they were introduced to their lecturers, they were told the college rules, they were given maps of the campus, and were told how the Cafeteria works. It was the beginning of college life for Lucky Atlega 'Sky' Molapo.

CHAPTER 4
WELCOME AND ROMANCE

n their first weekend at college, at midday on Saturday, Sky and her friends were chilling on chairs in the park-like area on campus, out of the women's hostels and near the library. A group of boy bullies accompanied by some girls unexpectedly came around the corner to where the girls were sitting, and began shouting insulting comments at them.

There were eleven boys who were known for being troublemakers on campus. Most were final-year students, or students who always failed their modules. The senior person in the group was a boy called 'Skherekhere', who was a tall ugly boy with scars on his face and head. He was smoking dagga and rumours were that he was a dangerous person who always had a knife in his pocket. The rumour also said his father was a car hijacker, and many believed that if your father was a criminal, you were likely to follow in your father's footsteps.

It was also said that Skherekhere was impossible to suspend because his father was notorious around

Siyabuswa where the college was situated, and he was a friend of some of the lecturers.

Some of the students said he once stabbed a person older than him with a knife at a tavern in Siyabuswa, but what was surprising was that no one saw Skherekhere with a knife, and no one witnessed the stabbing. Skherekhere had never been suspended from college, he didn't have a seriously bad record, and he hadn't failed any of his modules. Meanwhile his father was in prison for stealing cattle from the communities surrounding Siyabuswa to pay for his son's college tuition.

Skherekhere had a group of students who worshipped him, and on that Saturday, which was the 'welcoming day' for first-year students, he and his followers were walking around collecting first-year students – they were moving fast before security staff could see what was happening

Lee said sharply, "Skherekhere!" to let Sky and Lebo know he was coming. They stood up to try to run back to the hostel, but they were too late. Skherekhere and his crew blocked them. "Hey, hey, hey ... student card." Skherekhere said to Sky and Lala, who produced their cards, shaking and scared, and handed them to Skherekhere. "Ooh, newcomers! Come, come, come, follow the train." He told Sky and Lala to follow the first-year students who were walking in front of the bullies. Popla and Lee were scared of Skherekhere because of the rumours they had heard about him. They knew that every year, Skherekhere and his crew bullied the first-year students – and the scariest part was that every year the bullying was different. Popla and Lee were worried about what might happen to their roommates.

It was part of campus culture to 'welcome' first-year students, and the college did not encourage nor discourage the culture, as long as no one got hurt, and the college did not address the 'welcoming' culture as misconduct or punishable. At the same time, Security had to maintain order, no matter what was happening.

Skherekhere and his crew walked the students to the water taps behind the Cafeteria; Popla with Lee followed the crowd while their friends Sky and Lala were walked in front with other first-year students. "Against the wall," Skherekhere instructed the students to line up against the Cafeteria wall, facing the crowd. One of his boys stole a heavy-duty water pipe from a storeroom and sprayed the students until they were all soaking wet. They stood there helplessly, without saying anything. Skherekhere was scary. The crowd felt sorry for the first-years, and shouted, "No! Skherekhere, stop, it is enough!" In the meantime, Skherekhere and his crew were singing and shouting, "We baptise you in the name of the Father, the Son and the Holy Spirit." They didn't stop until Security showed up, and then they ran off in different directions.

Security did nothing because it was college culture, but they had to deal with the noise and commotion to maintain order on the campus. At the end of the day, it wasn't such a big deal, everyone was joking about it, and even the victims were laughing. Popla and Lee hugged their roommates, saying, "Welcome guys!"

Anyway, Skherekhere with his crew continued to be 'masupa' (powerful people) of the Kwandebele College campus, days passed and everyone forgot what had happened to the newcomers against the Cafeteria wall.

Then St Valentine's Day was approaching. Sky had never had a boyfriend, nor had she had any interest in dating. She didn't think it was necessary to have a boyfriend. Lala was just like Sky; their chitchat was all about school, jokes, the future, or they were there for each other during difficult days. They both had big dreams to live a big fat life. On the other hand, Popla and Lee were all about jumping from boy to boy. Popla was three years older than Sky and Lala, and Lee was two years older than Sky and Lala.

Sky and her roommates sat together in the Cafeteria for breakfast, lunch, and dinner, unless someone was attending class or had other plans. It was the same with Bongani with his roommates. One day he was alone in the Cafeteria because his roommates were late from soccer practice and were still showering before dinner. Bongani was also a soccer player but he had not gone for practice because he needed to study. He went to sit with Sky and her friends before his roommates joined him in the Cafeteria. "Hello …" he waved a greeting to the Room 16 girls. They greeted him in return, but Lee's greeting was the loudest, as if she wanted to attract attention to herself. Bongani greeted Lee again, and she responded with a smile. "Huu! Love is in the air!" said Popla. Sky and Lala did not take it seriously because Bongani was their friend – but they laughed along with the others.

Sky introduced Bongani to Popla and Lee and he asked if he could join them at their table. Popla noticed that Lee was charmed by Bongai, and she did not have a problem with that. Who can resist Bongani? He was indeed charming, tall and good looking, and he was sweet and polite.

Bongani spoke with what they described as a 'bedroom voice' – low and slow speaking. Lee was smitten, and while Popla accepted that Bongani was charming, he was not her type. Popla was interested in wild boys.

After a while, Bongani's friends came in the Cafeteria and joined their friend and the Room 16 girls. Bongani introduced them and they sat together, with Bongani entertaining the girls. Lee was more focused on him than on what he was saying.

The friends began sitting together often in the Cafeteria. Bongani had his eye on Lee, Joman on Lala, Small on Popla, and Itumeleng on Sky – they were matched four by four. It became an everyday thing and they became known in the college as Group Eight. They started as friends, and then they started dating. For Popla and Lee, falling for the guys was easy; they had done it many times. But for Sky and Lala, this was their first time dating, but they did enjoy Joman and Itumeleng, who were great guys, and were very attractive to girls.

Itumeleng and Sky were a very attractive match – he was beautiful with big black lips, and he was taller than Sky. Most of the girls in college were jealous of the Room 16 girls, and the boys were jealous of Bongani and his roommates, but at the same time, most students liked the Group Eight because they had that swag.

Itumeleng was also romantic; he was totally a gentlemen and was a dream catch to every girl on campus. Every day after classes, he would collect Sky to walk around the campus, they would buy chips and cold drink and eat together while relaxing in the park. On some days, they just relaxed together, far from everyone else, and talked sweet nothings to each other. On weekends, Sky would prepare a lunch and she and Itumeleng would go and have a picnic in the bushveld alongside the main road.

The girls also adopted the boy's rule of 'Injury to one is injury to all,' and often the girls would watch their boys at soccer practice, and the boys would support their girls at netball practice. But even though love was very much in the air, they did not forgot their main reason for being at college. The Group Eight students were responsible and they constantly reminded each other that education comes first, and they all loved education.

Itumeleng could also play guitar and he loved to play for Sky sometimes while chilling on the campus field. He was not interested in pursuing music as a career, but Sky was interested in learning to play guitar – it was a beautiful instrument to her eyes and it looked easy to play. Itumeleng appreciated Sky's love of music and he taught her how to play in their free time and on weekends when they were together. He was from an educated rich family, just like Bongani from the town of Kwamhlanga, about fifty kilometres south-west of Kwandebele College, and his father was a successful businessman, local radio station host, and he owned a driving school. His mother was an author of primary school educational books, and she was well-known for writing children's books in isiNdebele. She was also an ambassador of the isiNdebele culture around South Africa. Many girls did not only want to be with Itumeleng for his beauty and romantic spirit, but also because his parents were famous. David and Ntombi Manaka loved their boy; he was their only child and they wanted to raise him the best way possible.

One Saturday, when Group Eight was having lunch, Small suggested they go for a night out at Mzala Tavern, not far from the college and known to host celebrities and rich people. What was also appealing was that a variety of musicians came to play at the tavern every weekend.

This would be the first time for Sky and Lala to break campus rules, but they trusted their friends, especially Bongani, and they agreed to join the group that night. The question was how were they going to sneak out of campus and hide their identity at the tavern. The college students generally visited small taverns where they would not come face-to-face with lectures or hostel housekeepers. Kwandebele College was known to be strict about its rules and was successful in producing high status people such as principals, teachers, nurses, and lawyers. Gates closed at six o'clock, and no students were allowed to be outside after ten o'clock unless there was an emergency. Misconduct was punishable with three warnings followed by a suspension, depending on the seriousness of misconduct.

Some students, however, had ways to escape and enter the hostel after curfew without being seen, or they knew someone they could bribe with money or a half-jack of whisky to let them out and in. Students who did not have money or whisky could jump the fence at the back without being detected, where Skherekhere and his crew had opened a fence at the back beyond the pool area.

The lecturers' hostel on campus was situated at the front near the main gate. The hole in the fence was not easy to detect because it was cut from top to bottom, and it was in an area where Security didn't often patrol, and in any case, the students knew when Security patrolled.

To sneak out of hostel, students ran from wall to wall, timing the Security patrols and the one at the hostel entrance. Small was the mastermind for smuggling people to where ever they wanted to go on or out of campus at night. Some students were dating people from the area outside college, some wanted a night out at a tavern, and some were recruited by criminals to get involved in robberies, carjacking, or smuggling dagga at the college. They took advantage of students from poor families, but some were family members, and it was Small's responsibility to make sure they got in and out safely. Small was naturally bright and he didn't use illegal methods to smuggle people around and out of campus. He was a funny and chatty, and everyone knew him, from the Rector and lecturers, to all the staff and students, and people outside campus. Small looked innocent, but he was a smooth operator and you couldn't tell if he was telling lies.

It was easy for the Group Eight to sneak out with Small as the master planner. At eight-thirty sharp, the Group Eight students would meet behind the library. Small would negotiate with Security to smuggle them out in the back of the security bakkie, and collect them again at midnight.

After they heard Small explain the plan, they were quiet for few seconds, they looked at each other and laughed. "Whoever could have thought of that plan," said Sky, laughing. "Small is a man with a solution for everything!" They were all laughing. It was a good plan and they knew Small was the master of smuggling everything coming or going out or around the college. They agreed to the plan and went off to prepare for a night out. In Room 16, the girls were bathing, choosing clothes, trying them on, wanting to look beautiful for their boyfriends. The boys were doing the same.

At eight-thirty they were all behind the library waiting for transport. The security vehicle came slowly and stopped at a distance; Small went to the passenger side and gave the person a small plastic packet. He then waved his hand for the group to come; they ran and jumped into the back of the bakkie, and lay flat while the bakkie drove out of campus. After a few minutes it stopped. "Ok Small … you can jump out. Twelve o'clock sharp!" said the security person. They all jumped out. "Sure, Mdala," said Small.

It was a few minutes' walk to Mzala Tavern, which was a big white building with big green letters in bold, MZALA. It was quiet outside, but inside was loud with music playing, and people dancing, some were sitting at tables drinking and talking.

The band on stage was performing, and they noticed some of their lecturers dancing with students – it seemed as if some were dating. "*Welcome to hell*," said Small. He had been coming to Mzala quite frequently, but hiding it from Group Eight. He knew that nothing would happen to Group Eight if they snuck out because several lecturers also has secrets to hide; they were dating students and sneaking them out of campus to Mzala or taking them to their homes. These lecturers were paying the price by doing favours for Small so he would not leak their secrets to Rector Nkadimeng, who liked Small for his natural bright-ness and his soccer skills. No one could touch Small when the Rector was around.

The group booked a table and ordered drinks. Bongani, Sky and Lala had not been exposed to alcohol in their lives and they chose to drink sodas or juice. This was a first experience for all of them, except Small, who was a chancer, and who always won in the chances he took. They enjoyed themselves that night, and they continued visiting Mzala until it was exam time.

Sky was usually the one who suggested going out because Mzala encouraged local musicians and solo singers to perform. One day she told her friends that she want to perform at Mzala. Bongani and Lala knew she could sing but the others were not sure. They only know that Itumeleng was teaching her to play guitar and she was playing it very well, in fact, she was playing like a professional and she was already better than Itumeleng. She would borrow his guitar to play it at the pool for Group Eight while they relaxed, and other students would gather around to hear her play.

CHAPTER 5
MUSIC AT MZALA

As time went on, she started writing new songs in her free time and played to the students on campus. Soon the lecturers too, realised that she had talent. Lala and Bongani would tell the others about Sky's singing in the school choir, when she was not around to hear them. Although they had doubts, the Group Eight students – apart from Lala and Bongani who believed in Sky – chose to support her because Group Eight believed in their team. It was not easy to get a gig at Mzala if you were not a known local musician because you were going to play for people of a high calibre, and the club had its reputation to uphold. The group suggested that Small could talk to his connection to organise a gig for Sky. As he couldn't say no to a challenge, Small spoke to one of the lecturers, Mr Godfrey Kekana, who was a friend of the man who owned Mzala, Vincent Mo'Russia. On campus, the students called their lecturer Sir Kekana, but on the streets they called him 'Godfather'. He had become friends with Vincent Mo'Russia after spending a lot of time at Mzala over weekends and during the week after work. Godfather was probably an alcoholic.

Vincent Mo'Russia was a tall well-built man, dark in colour and scary, but he was decent, and he helped out when the community was in need and he was respected for that. No one knew his surname – everyone called him Vincent Mo'Russia – and no one knew where he came from or anything about his family. He had arrived in the eighties to settle in Siyabuswa. The rumours said he was from Free State and he had run away in the riots of the seventies, and that was why he spoke SeSotho. He soon established businesses and he now owned taxis, a farm, and Mzala Tavern – where leading politicians, musicians, chiefs, and others in Kwandebele's high society made a point of visiting.

Godfather did connect Sky with Vincent Mo'Russia for a gig, but he wanted Sky to come and play one song during the week after classes as a trial. According to Small, if Sky could impress Vincent Mo'Russia, she would be given a gig that weekend. Sky's friends went with her to her appointment, for the sake of safety and also for the excitement of it. The appointment was on a Wednesday afternoon after classes. Sky practised hard and every afternoon she would go to the pool and sing and play guitar for the crowd as if it was as relaxed as usual, but Group Eight knew she was seriously practising.

Wednesday came and Sky and the group went to meet Vincent Mo'Russia. Godfather had offered to drive them there, mainly because he could then enjoy a few bottles of

'Zamalek' while he was there. At Mzala, Vincent Mo'Russia was outside. "Hey Mister," was Godfather's greeting to Vincent Mo'Russia, who responded, "Godfather, brother from another mother, how you doing?" Godfather then introduced his companions and pointed out Sky who wanted a gig in his tavern. Vincent Mo'Russia greeted her, and showed them all inside. "You can all sit here. Marry, bring my friends some drinks," he instructed one of his workers.

Marry brought guava juice for all of them. "No, no, no … my friend, you know this is not my stuff," said Godfather, who was not there for juice or to see Sky play. He wanted to drink. "Marry bring my friend Zamalek," Vincent Mo'Russia was laughing as he instructed Marry. He was pleased Godfather had brought him new talent; he believed that for his business to boom, he must always have new talent at Mzala. People in high society do not want to see the same musicians every time they visit the tavern.

They turned their attention to Sky. Vincent Mo'Russia was thinking that she looked too young to sing and drive the crowd crazy, but although he was a scary-looking person, Vincent Mo'Russia believed everyone should have a chance. He asked Sky if she could sing and she responded by saying, "If I cannot put a smile on your face, I will curse the day I was born." She sounded very confident. The group looked at each other nervously, but Sky was relaxed. Vincent Mo'Russia chuckled for a few moments without responding, and deep inside he was starting to believe that Sky was the person he was looking for to boom his business. He showed Sky the stage with the wave of a hand without saying anything. She stood up with energy, picked up Itumeleng's guitar, and walked onto the stage. She stood looking at Vincent Mo'Russia, Godfather, her friends, and Marry and a few of the workers, she moved the guitar into position, placed her fingers on the strings, breathed in and out, strummed a couple of times to get the pitch, and then she started singing a song that she had written earlier that week, but that her friends had not yet heard. Her song was called, 'I hear music everywhere.'

> *Tell me to stop singing and you'll be tearing my life*
> *   into pieces*
> *stop loving me because you don't want me to sing*
> *then it's ok I won't cry*
> *cut my tongue I will continue to sing in my head for*
> *   as long as I live …*
> *you cannot stop me from my dream*
> *(Chorus)*
> *I hear music everywhere …*
> *music is everywhere …*
> *even canary birds sing beautiful music every day*

She continued to sing and strum the guitar. Marry stopped dusting, she watched Sky with her hands on her mouth. The two other workers had also stopped cleaning, and Vincent Mo'Russia, Godfather, and the group were smiling from ear to ear. It was obvious that Sky had her gig. Vincent Mo'Russia's answer was already yes, but he asked Sky to play another song. She smiled and fixed her voice again, and then started strumming the guitar, before

singing another song she had written, called 'Rise and rise.'
It was a song that motivated her when she was down.

> *I 'wanna' be who I 'wanna' be*
> *I will be who I 'wanna' be*
> *I 'wanna' fly and I will fly sky high where eagles fly*
> *(Chorus)*
> *Rise and rise queen until witches get tired*
> *for you are the queen …*
> *Rise and rise until mountains fall, for you are a diva*

Sky's friends were surprised; it was clear her talent was
growing every day, and her new songs were a hit. From the
moment she started singing, no one had touched their
drinks, even Godfather had forgotten his Zamalek on the
table. Vincent Mo'Russia was smiling broadly when Sky
came back to the table. "That was nice music girl," he said,
patting her on the shoulder. He was tearful, and he looked
down and then slowly he looked up again. He said to them,
"People don't know who I am; they say all kinds of false
things about me. You will be the first to know me, lucky
hey?" He smiled; they looked at each other and at him.

He continued, "My name is Gift Mofokeng from Free
State. My mother died when I was young and my father
moved to Johannesburg together with us, he was running
away from the memories of his wife passing, and he was a
singer, just like you Sky. He played guitar as well; it was his
source of income to take care of us. He played at the
station and came home late every day, with bread for us."
Vincent Mo'Russia kept quiet for a few seconds, he then

breathed very deeply and continued. "He was killed, stabbed thirteen times in the chest for those crumbs he made every day to take care of us. I had to be a man at the age of fourteen and take care of my siblings. I then ended up coming to Siyabuswa to start a new life and forget the past, but I never forget where I come from." He told them that short story that left them with many questions, but it was so sad that no one asked questions. They thought maybe the story would continue. But then Vincent Mo'Russia said, "Sky, I will be happy if you will come to sing in the 'Sunday Chillas' session this Sunday, from midday."

She jumped up high with delight, and her friends were happy and jumping around too, hugging her, and shouting, "Yes baby, you made it!" and other excited outbursts. Godfather was also happy for Sky.

They left with smiles. Their friend was going to perform at Mzala, the famous big tavern in Siyabuswa that hosts the region's VIPs. Vincent Mo'Russia promised Group Eight VIP seats inside with all those famous people. His story about his sad childhood touched their hearts and they swore they would go to their graves keeping his secret. Godfather also kept the secret, and his friendship with Vincent Mo'Russia grew stronger. They all agreed to continue calling him Vincent Mo'Russia, because people would ask questions if they called him Gift.

On Saturday that week, Sky was playing at the pool for students, in preparation for 'Sunday Chillas' at Mzala. She had written many songs since her school days when most of her songs were gospel, but at college, she wrote songs for all types of music.

For 'Sunday Chillas' she was going to sing her new songs, but the question was, was she going to shake the crowd? On Sunday morning, Sky woke up and drank a glass of warm water with a spoon of spirit vinegar to 'clean' her voice. She wasn't going to talk much that day, to save her voice for the performance.

They kept it a secret on campus that Sky was going to perform at Mzala because if Rector Nkadimeng found out, he would tell Principal Mahlangu who would tell Sky's parents. That was not going to be good news for Sefako and Baby; they raised their daughter to be a teacher, not a musician.

It's not a good thing when parents choose a destiny for their children, but in the nineties, older people believed that everything they said to children would be good for their futures, regardless of whether their children had different dreams.

Later that Sunday, Sky and her friends set off for Mzala in a vehicle that had been organised by Small with one of his security guard friends on campus – someone he regularly supplied with dagga. They arrived an hour before Sky was due to perform. Being in a VIP area was a first-time experience for the group, and they were awestruck in the presence of famous people, radio hosts, and musicians. Some musicians were already on stage, and others were relaxing. Vincent Mo'Russia was running the business, and he was anxious about Sky's first performance.

Sky and her friends were well taken care of by a Mzala waiter, and Godfather also joined them to support Sky. Just before it was time for Sky to sing, she prepared the guitar, and tuned it, and then went on stage. Vincent Mo'Russia had prepared everything. She walked up to the microphone, positioned it, fixed her voice, and took a deep breath. Before people could ask who was that on stage, she started to sing her song called, 'My name is Lucky Sky'.

My mother named me Lucky and I feel so lucky to
    love music
I pray with music
express feelings with music
show love with music
I am a music slave chained to my guitar
my blood runs deep through veins with music that
    people never heard
music that hit deep in to the core of my heart
and opened veins that were about to block
(Chorus)
If you don't know my name
call me Lucky cause I feel lucky to love music
you can call me Sky the dreamer just like my friends
    call me
famous for singing good songs
no joke I sing baby
you will cry for more

It was a great song and people stood up clapping and cheering. Some of the artists were amazed at Sky's strong velvety voice, but jealousy was buried deep inside. She was just a young girl without status, but she sang better than many people who had been training for years. The crowd went crazy when she stopped and called for more, which was good; she was going to sing a second song anyway. Vincent Mo'Russia looked at Sky and nodded as he raised his glass of whisky to her. He was satisfied with the way she had started. While he was still watching, Sky started another song. It was a song about her boyfriend, no one had heard it before, except Itumeleng. She played it for him when they were chilling together and he loved it.

> *At first he was a friend*
> *then it was a joke*
> *it started to be serious*
> *then it was love*
> *I was lost but he found me*
> *I never loved before but he loved me*
> *carry me on his shoulder but feel more comfortable*
> *   inside his hand*
> *wrapped his arms around me like I'm a small baby*
> *I feel all the love inside him.*
> *(Chorus)*
> *I love this man to death*
> *no Benjamins can change my mind*
> *my love for him is worth any dollar bills*

In no time couples were dancing, Popla with Small, Lee with Bongani, and Lala with Jovan, while Itumeleng watched Sky's performance and blushed. Godfather was already wasted and was dancing with every woman who was willing to dance with him – they were not interested in Godfather, but the women in the club knew that he bought lots of booze.

After the performance, Sky went down to sit with her friends, and people came to their table and asked a lot of questions she could not answer; she did not want all this to end up in her parent's ears. Vincent Mo'Russia went to the table when he saw what was happening; he realised that Sky was performing without her parents' knowledge. You can't fool Vincent Mo'Russia – he's a man who knows everything before it happens.

He took out his wallet and gave Sky five hundred rand as payment for her performance. She didn't want to take the money because she sang to satisfy her soul – to her it was all about having fun at that moment, she hadn't thought about making lots of money from her music. She was studying teaching to have a job to satisfy her parents; she hadn't considered music as a career. Music was a hobby that she would do part time while working as a teacher, but now she realised she could make a living with her music. She froze; she didn't know what to do or say when Vincent Mo'Russia handed her the money and everyone was surprised. Small was a quick thinker. He pushed Sky's hand to take the money, and Sky took it, shaking. Five hundred rand was a lot in the nineties; enough to buy schoolbooks and have fun with friends with the change. She would save some of the money. "Girl, you don't work for free in this tavern. You work, I pay," Vincent Mo'Russia told Sky after she accepted the money. He knew that if he paid, she would come back, and if she came back, she would bring a crowd because the people loved her music. It was going to be a win-win for them both. "Same time next week if you want more," he said, and turned and walked away from the table. She shouted after him, "I am coming back," and he looked back, smiled, and gave her a thumbs up.

Group Eight went back to campus, and the next day, students were talking about Sky's performance at Mzala. The group had thought it was going to be a secret but how could it be when other students also visited Mzala. And Godfather talks too much when he's drunk – he would give away secrets, even about his own family.

It was only a matter of time before Sefako and Baby found out about Sky and Mzala. She just crossed her finger and hoped it wouldn't reach them too soon because there was no way that she was going to stop performing at Mzala once she had realised that her hobby could be a career.

That week she had asked Itumeleng a question while they were chilling and eating chips next to a café on campus. Sky was calling him 'Mfanaka'. "Mfanaka, do you think I can be a musician?" She asked. "You can be what you want to be," Itumeleng answered. She kept quiet while eating chips and looking at Itumeleng. Then after a few seconds she said in a soft voice, "I thought you were going to be clear in your answer." Immediately Itumeleng responded, "You are a musician, Sky. If what you say actually means you want to leave college, the answer is 'no', but if what you're saying is that you want to have music as your career after college, then the answer is 'yes'." He knew Sky always wanted clear and honest answers. She laughed with her mouth closed because she had taken a mouthful of chips. "Don't be silly! I won't drop out, my parents would disown me if I did that." It was obvious that Itumeleng would support Sky in everything; he was also her shoulder to lean on.

She continued to perform without her parents knowing that she wanted to pursue music as her career or that she was performing at Mzala. Sky and the rest of Group Eight did not know that Rector Nkadimeng and Principal Mahlangu already knew, but Rector Nkadimeng asked Principal Mahlangu to keep it a secret. He also convinced Principal Mahlangu that Sky was a bright student in class, and that she could easily handle both her studies and music at the same time. He reminded Principal Mahlangu that his parents had forced him to go to college when he had always wanted to be a soccer star. Principal Mahlangu also knew that Sky had been a good singer in high school, and they both agreed to keep it a secret.

Sky was lucky that Rector Nkadimeng and Principal Mahlangu both believed that children must follow their own dreams, just as Principal Mahlangu and his wife had allowed their son, Thulani, to become a soldier instead of following a career in agriculture.

At the end of the first year, Sky passed all her modules with flying colours, and Lala and the others in Group Eight also passed all their modules. Sefako and Baby were happy with the results, and they saved enough money to buy new clothes for Sky when she returned to college for the second year, to show their pride and appreciation.

Mr and Mrs Monkoe were also happy with their daughter's results. Lala wrote a letter to her father's employers, Mr and Mrs Williams, to tell them about her results. They were so pleased they added another ten per cent to the fifty per cent they were already sponsoring.

That December, Sky could not perform at Mzala because she was home, spending the festive season with her parents. They always came first. Through the year, she had spent most of her time at college, sometimes skipping a visit home to perform at Mzala. What she missed most, though, was spending time with Itumeleng. He was her first lover – and she and Lala would talk about how much they missed their boyfriends when they were home. But they reminded themselves that it was only for a month.

CHAPTER 6
SINGING FOR THE COLLEGE

t was January 1995 and Sky was going back to college for her second year. Before she left, she put one thousand rand in a jar that her parents put money they were saving in. It was a portion of her savings from money she made performing at Mzala; she didn't want to give the money directly to her parents as that would lead to many questions she didn't want to answer. They would not appreciate her doing music part time. Sky had secretly put money in the jar every time she had come home since she started singing at Mzala.

She kissed her parents goodbye and shouted for Lala to come out so they could walk to the bus stop that was also a taxi stop. They would catch a taxi to Siyabuswa. Even though it was not on the taxi route, many of the taxi drivers recognised Sky from Mzala and would sometimes offer to drop them off at the college entrance.

When Sky and Lala returned to college, they were ready to go into second year, but Popla and Lee were starting their final year.

The next morning there was a knock on the door of Room 16, which was unexpected. It was Mrs Mmapule Nchabeleng the Hostel Housekeeper. She spoke to Sky, "Rector Nkadimeng wants to see you at ten o'clock." She left without waiting for Sky to respond. The girls asked themselves a lot of questions about this development, but they advised Sky not to worry; she had only returned the day before and no one could remember anything that had happened that could make the Rector angry. And though Sky did not have a record of bad behaviour, the issue of performing at Mzala was the main topic of conversation among the girls.

"Naah girls, maybe Rector is in love," Popla teased Sky. "Oh no girl, don't even go there!" Sky responded. Everyone laughed, but the question was still not answered. The girls told the boys about the summons, and Group Eight prepared themselves for anything. After all, 'Injury to one is injury to all.'

At ten o'clock sharp she knocked on Rector Nkadimeng's door. "Come in, Lucky, have a seat," Rector called to her. She came in, greeted Rector Nkadimeng, and sat down. "Good morning Sir, I heard you were wanting to see me."

Rector Nkadimeng explained why he had asked Sky to come to his office. "Next week is the graduation. I have often heard you sing at the pools. Can you come and sing for our graduates? Eee, the college doesn't have funds to pay you, but we can offer you the college hall to play in anytime you want because I have noticed you love music. Is that enough?" He didn't reveal that he knew about her singing at Mzala.

Sky responded immediately. "Ok Sir, no problem I will of course sing at the graduation. And thank you Sir, for offering the hall."

"Ok, you will be responsible for the college hall. Everyone who needs to use the hall must come to you to book it; here are the keys, Lucky." He handed her the college hall keys and the register for bookings. He then added, "Another thing, Lucky. Why don't you contest for the Student Representative Council?"

"Sir, I want to focus on my studies," Sky answered.

Rector Nkadimeng nodded, but he realised she was lying. The reason Sky didn't want to be on the Student Representative Council was because she wanted to focus more on music than on college issues. The Rector explained why he asked that question. "Principal Mahlangu told me a lot about you. He said you were voted onto the Learners Representative Council right through your high school years. I asked myself why you hadn't contested to be on the Student Representative Council. But I understand. You can be dismissed. Just prepare for next week's graduation."

"Ok, Sir. Thank you," Sky replied and left his office to join Group Eight in the Cafeteria where they were waiting to hear about her visit to the Rector's office.

She sat down and explained everything that Rector Nkadimeng had said, that she would be singing at the grad-uation the next week, and she told them she had been given the task of college hall keeper.

Small immediately asked, "How much are they going to pay?" Group Eight laughed then Sky said, "Boy, please!

You love money, you can be my manager!" They continued to laugh, and then Sky explained that the college would not pay because they are short of funds, and explained Rector Nkadimeng's offer to her to use the hall as long as she was a student at Kwandebele College. The group was happy about that arrangement and started planning gigs in the college hall, even discussing charging an entrance fee.

As Sky was still using Itumeleng's guitar, she decided she needed to get her own. Itumeleng was not happy because he wanted Sky to play his guitar, but as always, he respected her decision. They planned that the next day, Sky and her friends would go to Pretoria to buy a new guitar with some of Sky's savings.

The following day they took a taxi to Pretoria, which was a long trip of about two hours from Siyabuswa. They alighted at Proes Street in the city centre, at about ten in the morning. Only Itumeleng and Small were familiar with Pretoria as they were both from Kwamhlanga, which was not far from Pretoria. They had been into Pretoria with their parents on the occasional shopping trips, and Itumeleng was familiar with the area because he had often visited his cousin who had been studying at the University of Pretoria. Small frequently visited his father in Mamelodi West; he fixed shoes and watches at Bosman Station where he worked at a small table, and sometimes Small would go and help him. Small's parents had separated when he was young, but Mr Masango was doing everything he could to give Small a better education.

Itumeleng took the lead and they went to buy Sky a new guitar. On the corner of Van der Walt and Schoeman streets was a music shop where Itumeleng's parents had bought his guitar. They entered the shop and began the process of choosing a nice guitar for Sky, who knew exactly what she wanted. It was a waste of time for the group to choose anything, because at the end of the day, Sky wants what Sky wants.

After about thirty minutes of looking around the shop, Sky saw a shiny black guitar in the corner, and next to it was a guitar bag. She pointed. "How much is that one, Sir?" she asked the sales person. The group turn and looked to where Sky was pointing as they were surprised at Sky's reaction.

"Wow!" they said as one voice. The guitar was affordable and Sky bought it.

The friends then went to see a movie in Arcadia, and later returned to the city centre, to sit in the Union Buildings park, take pictures of each other, and kiss and say sweet nothings. But Sky was telling Itumeleng that one day she wanted to come and play for a big crowd at the Union Buildings.

The group wanted Sky to play immediately; they knew she could sing without any preparation, but Sky only wanted to open her guitar for the college graduation. At that moment, she only wanted to bond with Itumeleng after their long December holidays of not seeing each other.

When it was time to go back to college, they walked to Marabastad Station to catch a taxi to Siyabuswa. They arrived back late after the gates were closed, but they didn't have to worry because they had Small with them, who organised a security patrol vehicle to smuggle them back onto campus.

The following day at about four o'clock, Group Eight was chilling at the soccer field, chatting about the previous day's trip, Sky was quiet. "Hey girl, what is wrong? Why are you so quiet?" Lee asked Sky.

"I'm thinking of my gig next week at graduation," Sky responded. The group was surprised, they looked at each other. They had thought everything was in order, and she had her new guitar.

Sky turned to Small. "Small, can you please organise me a bass guitar player, a keyboard player, and a drums player. They must have their own instruments."

"Yes I can. I know someone who plays bass guitar and I will find the others for you, Sky," he responded without asking questions.

Realising that her friends didn't understand, she explained with a laugh, "I want to perform at the graduation with a band."

Some of her friends thought she was perfect performing alone, and they started a conversation about the idea. Itumeleng, Bongani and Lala believed it was a good idea, but in the end, the conclusion was to let Sky do whatever she decided and they would support her.

Small did what he was asked by Sky and went home that weekend to organise a bass guitar player from his *kasi*, Kwamhlanga. Her name was Queen Funde and she regularly played at Kwamhlanga Complex in a band with her brother Andy Funde, who was an acoustic guitar player, Kabelo 'KB' Metsena, who was a keyboard player, and

Segopotso Komane, who was on drums. They always played SeSotho songs.

Itumeleng also knew the band because they had all attended the same school, Kwamhlanga High, which was next to the old Kwandebele parliament. Queen, Andy, KB, and Segopotso had played in the school band; they were all from poor families and had not been able to continue their studies after matric. They decided to use their music skills to form a band and play at Kwamhlanga Complex to make a living. People gave them money when they played, and they also played at weddings, parties, and schools at matric dances.

Queen was happy to help Sky in her performance at the graduation, but the band refused. They had to earn an income, and they didn't want to waste their time performing for free. In the end, Sky convinced the band to perform at the graduation for free, and in return, she would perform with them at Mzala. She then convinced Vincent Mo'Russia to allow her to perform with the band. He agreed, but he said he wouldn't pay them – he would only pay Sky, who was the person he hired.

Sky was also fine with that arrangement. She just needed Vincent Mo'Russia's permission. She would share what she was paid with the band. They accepted Sky's offer. It was a win-win for all of them; the band would gain popularity by playing at Kwandebele College and then at Mzala, and they would earn an income. As it was, Mzala was a famous tavern and no band would refuse to play there; it was known to host the big guns.

Sky let Rector Nkadimeng know that she would

performing with a band at the graduation ceremony and asked him to accommodate them on the campus for a few days. He agreed and asked Mrs Nchabeleng to organise accommodation for the band.

Small organised a vehicle to collect the band and their instruments from Kwamhlanga and bring them to college. They were given accommodation in the general workers' hostel for two days. As soon as Sky's classes ended, they started practising, and they worked together for six hours. It was difficult to start with as the band had their own style and Sky wanted to play her style. In the end, they came up with something that would make people happy. It was important for them all to deliver a good performance because not only students and lecturers would attend the graduation, but also many guests of the graduates and the college.

They were going to play five songs nonstop with Sky, Queen and Andy as singers, while also playing their instruments.

The day of graduation came. Once all the graduates had received their diplomas, it was time for the band to play. Sky's friends were sitting at the back with other students, while the graduates were in front with their family members, and on the stage was the Rector, other dignitaries, and lecturers.

The band was set up on the right hand side of the stage. The band was confident. They had seen that Sky was a great singer and guitar player, and Sky was also happy with the band's performance. They clearly had a lot of experience performing.

"Please welcome Sky and the band. They are going to play five songs," the Programme Director announced.

They stood up and picked up their instruments, and positioned their microphones. Sky took a deep breath, fixed her voice as usual, looked across at the other band players, who winked as a sign of readiness. She started with a song they had written together called 'Never look back.' But before she could start, the Group Eight members and other students started screaming, to boost her morale. The song had no lead singer – all three of the singers sang together.

> *Run baby run*
> *never look back*
> *run like you've been chased by a boogie man*
> *run baby run never look back*
> *run faster to catch your dreams*
> *dreams run faster than a fast car*
> *don't let them run faster than you baby*
> *catch those dreams now or never*
> *let your college days count and make it happen*
> *(Chorus)*
> *run baby run*
> *let your college days count*
> *and make it happen (3x)*

It was a beautiful song that was directed at the graduates who were possibly questioning if they would ever catch their dreams.

When the song ended, Segopotso played his drums softly until the next song started, and then played his drums like a crazy man, shaking his head to the beat of the song.

The second song was 'Roses bloom' was followed by 'Kings and Queens' and then 'Missing you already'. The last song made everyone in the hall cry. It was 'African child'. Sky sang solo.

Waking up in the morning without breakfast
I never had dinner last night
don't know if I will eat lunch today
wake up in the morning to fetch water at the river
*   Moutse with hunger eating my stomach*
the river so clean I can see my reflection
but I can't see it because I'm hoping I will find food
*   when I go back home maybe someone dropped*
*   their last night's leftovers*
From the river walking back home passing kids going
*   to school*
I can't go with them
I had to find a job to support my siblings
life turned me into a mother
cursing the day I was born
walking up the hill with a bucket full of water on
*   my head*
appreciate the little you have in life
I wish a genie was not a myth and get that lamp …
*   rub it and get three wishes to better my life*
who knows,
maybe the genie would be going to be on holiday
maybe I can still believe in God
never tried Him anyway
I heard people saying God listens but takes long to
*   answer*

I will have to wait
God is my last hope

After every verse, the bass guitar would go 'ding-ding, ding-ding, ding-ding ...' and the organ would go 'ting-ting, ting-ting, ting-ting ...'

Sky sang softly and slowly at first, and then she came in high, and then went low and slow again. The crowd was on its feet, clapping and shouting, and from the back, they were whistling and calling Sky's name. She had written the song a while back, but hadn't sung it in public as she was not sure about it. She had decided to play it that day with the band, and it turned out to be the song the crowd loved the most out of the five songs.

After the performance and when graduation was over, everyone wanted to take pictures with Sky and the band. The band was surprised by the professionalism of Sky's performance, and Rector Nkadimeng was so pleased he even offered to organise a vehicle to take the band back home.

It was the band's first performance in a college, and they felt it was special; graduations were clearly one of a kind. As from the next weekend, Sky would play with the band at Mzala. The problem was that the band lived forty kilometres from the area and they would not have a chance to practise together unless Sky could convince Vincent Mo'Russia to accommodate the band.

The band had a mixed tape that they used to try to get record deals, but every recording studio had rejected their mixed tape. Sky took it to use to negotiate with Vincent Mo'Russia. He wasn't convinced about the band, but he

had heard about their performance with Sky at the graduation, and he knew Sky wanted to be on stage with them, so
it was a done deal. He agreed to accommodate the band in
the tavern's back rooms that he rented out and where his
workers stayed when they worked late.

Group Eight was living a fat fabulous life; they had
their own table in the Cafeteria, VIP seats at Mzala, and
they were famous on campus and around Siyabuswa. The
taxi drivers dropped them at the college gate even though
was not on a taxi route. They were recognised by the
Rector and the lecturers, and were known to the VIP visitors to Mzala, all because of Lucky Atlega 'Sky' Molapo.

It was still January and Skherekhere had not forgotten
to play his part 'welcoming' newcomers to college. Even
though Sky and Lala had not forgotten their experience the
previous year, they attended the 'welcoming' of the
newcomers. This year, Skherekhere and his crew painted
the newcomers with a black paint that could be washed off.
Then, like people from initiation schools, they had to run
around the campus singing struggle songs. It was funny and
the madness lasted for fifteen minutes until Security came
to disperse the crowd.

Sky and the band started to practice a lot using the
college hall, and sometimes at Mzala. She was spending a
lot of time with the band and Group Eight was not happy.
Sky hadn't changed her behaviour towards her friends, she
just didn't have the time for them that she had had before.
She was focusing on her music and her studies, and had
only a little time for her friends.

Itumeleng suffered a lot as he was used to spending
time with his girlfriend. He became jealous when Sky was

practising with the band or performing, but the group gave him a lot of support as his friends. And even though the group was not happy, at the end of the day they understood; she was following her dreams. But still, Itumeleng could not accept it. Sometimes it felt as if Queen and the band were trying to take Sky away from them, and then Small regretted introducing Sky to the band. Tensions built up between Group Eight and the band, and Sky was caught in the middle. She always wanted peace to prevail between her friends and the band, and she tried to please them all, especially her boyfriend, while also focusing on her studies. She could not afford to lose her friends, they meant everything to her, and they supported her a lot. She loved Itumeleng so much, and yet the band was her passport to her dreams.

One day the Student Representative Counsel asked her to do something for Rector Nkadimeng on his birthday, which was approaching. Sky did not have any problem with that as Rector Nkadimeng was a good person who was loved by every student on the campus. He was strict but fair and down-to-earth. If you went to him with a problem, he would do what he could to help. Many students had been to him with their personal problems, and he had been caring and helpful.

The Student Representative Counsel did not have a specific plan; they knew Sky would have a plan complete with surprises, which proved to be true when she organised a celebration in the college hall on Valentine's Day in advance of the Rector's birthday surprise.

Two weeks before Valentine's Day, Sky stood on a table in the Cafeteria and told the students she and her crew were organising a Valentine's Day celebration. She announced that everyone must wear red and white and come as couples to the hall, holding red roses. She didn't tell them what would happen. She said they would not be allowed in without the right outfits, a rose, and a partner.

Sky was beautiful and popular, and she always made things happen. On Valentine's Day, students flocked to the hall to see what the big surprise would be. Sky then came in with her guitar and started singing and playing love songs. The students were dancing to the soft music that changed their mood to love mode. It was so special that if students didn't have a partner, they immediately asked someone for a date to be allowed inside the hall. Sky played R&B soul music nonstop, and only paused to drink water. The playlist was songs she had written – Sky was known not to play music by other musicians. She was a musician and a songwriter.

Sky then came up with a plan for Rector Nkadimeng's birthday surprise. The Student Representative Counsel organised a big cake from a local bakery, which they bought with students' donations. She then asked Group Eight to organise fifty students who sang in church or in choirs and were interested in being part of the birthday surprise party, to meet the next day after classes in the hall. The following day she met with the fifty students and they practised singing for Rector Nkadimeng's surprise party.

The following week on Friday, students gathered at the pool and the big cake was brought in. The surprise wasn't going to be very big, but it would be memorable. Sky and the choir that had been organised by Group Eight gathered in a group, and a student was sent to Rector Nkadimeng to call him to the pool area urgently as there was a serious fight going on. Sky positioned herself at the microphone and connected her guitar to the speakers, took a deep breath, fixed her voice, and waited for the signal she would be given when Rector Nkadimeng arrived. He came running behind the student who was sent to call him. He was struggling to keep up, the poor man had a big stomach and was in his late fifties, but he was doing the best he could. Just as he rounded the corner, Sky started to sing the first lines of a song she had written for the occasion, called 'Birthday Song'.

> *Your Roses wanna put a smile on your face*
> *happy birth to you Sir*
> *your Roses appreciate the love and care*
> *may God bless you with more days*
> *God bless this day a legend was born*
> *today and forever your Roses will continue to honour*
> *   and respect you*
> *The choir came in with lots of energy, singing the*
> *   chorus.*
> *You roar like a lion*
> *sing like a bird*
> *and you flow like a river*
> *happy birthday*
> *you're a winter watchman*

They continued to sing the chorus while Sky led and played 'Rose', the name she had given to her guitar because roses are a symbol of love, and she loved her guitar.

After the song, Rector Nkadimeng was very happy. They gave him his cake to eat together with the lecturers as it was not going to be enough for all the students. Rector Nkadimeng gave a short speech to thank the students. He mentioned that he had never had a surprise party before and he felt appreciated.

Then it was over, but the students wanted to hear Sky play and they begged for more once the Rector had left with his cake. She was happy to continue playing. She often tried new songs to hear the students' opinions of her music, which had always been positive.

The year went on for Sky and Group Eight, and once again, Sky passed with flying colours and Sefako and Baby were very proud of their little girl.

Group Eight all passed at the end of the year, though Popla and Lee had finished their final year and would be graduating. The next year was going to be difficult for Group Eight; two of their members would be leaving their boyfriends and friends. Popla was going back home to Delmas in Mpumalanga and Lee was going home to Wolmaransstad, known as 'Wolis', situated in North West Province. It was sad for Small and Bongani, but they were comforted to have the other members of Group Eight.

At midday on Saturday after graduation, Popla introduced her parents to Group Eight and they said their goodbyes. They helped to pack her belongings and take them to the car where they said goodbye for the last time. Lee's parents were too old to travel the long distance and had not been able to attend her graduation. Lee's brother came to fetch her the next morning, and she tearfully said her goodbyes to her friends and Bongani. They hugged with the hope that they would meet again soon.

"Sky, fly baby, I want to see you on television one day girl," Lee said to Sky as they hugged and kissed again. Sky didn't have words. She smiled and waved, and Lee climbed in the car and they drove away.

Group Eight was no longer Group Eight – it was down to Group Six.

CHAPTER 7
SKY'S RISE

1996 was the third and last year at college for the remaining members of Group Eight; they continued calling themselves Group Eight, even though they were only six. They believed their Group Eight relationships would continue and that Popla and Lee would always be in their hearts. They talked about them a lot, remembering the first day they met.

In those days, cell phones were scarce and pay phones were seldom available in the Siyabuswa area so the only means of communication was letter-writing. The post office was an important place in the nineties, and sending letters was a cheap method to communicate with loved ones.

Kwandebele College was going to close at the end of term in 1996 for political reasons. The new South African government that came into power in 1994, disbanded the homelands of the apartheid days and established nine provinces. Kwandebele College was being incorporated into the University of Mpumalanga based in Nelspruit. All students enrolled in Kwandebele College had an opportunity to continue their studies at the University of Mpumalanga, or with another college of their choice. With no new students coming in, Sky and Lala were the only occupants of Room 16.

One day in the Cafeteria the group was having lunch minding their own business, when they received a letter from the mail office, addressed to Room 16. It was from Lerato – Lee. They gathered around to hear her news. Lala started to read and the letter:

"Hello my friends, this is your friend Lee. Anyone who receives this letter must please read it together with everyone and by everyone I mean Group Eight; I miss all of you people. Since I left, this is the first time you hear from me. I was still adjusting to be home and was busy helping my parents at the supermarket full time. Two weeks after I got home my mother had a stroke and I had to help my father with administration. Things changed at home. My brother was promoted to Johannesburg and is now living there. I stay alone with my parents and everything is on me now, but I am trying my best to handle the situation. I miss sneaking out of college to Mzala, going to Pretoria … all those funny chats we had in Room 16. Ooh! I miss my bed, those days at the pool having fun, Sky playing guitar, our table at Cafeteria, I miss everything about Group Eight, and Bongani I love you. Please take care of my man. I hope I will see you soon and I hope no woman already took my space. Sky never stop singing your music. It is so good, and after you have dropped your first album, I must be the first to know. Lala, you will be a good teacher. I wish you luck in your studies. Bongani and Itumeleng, I wish you well in your Law careers good luck.

Joman and Small, you must be comedians, guys, I always remember how you were so entertaining. To all of you may God bless you. I heard the college is going to close, so please people, you must all pass. When I sent you this letter, I also sent to Popla. I hope she is doing well my friend. I hope that one day we will meet again, I love you all. Goodbye."

The group was happy to hear that their friend was doing well, even though the news about her mother was not good. Bongani was most excited to know that Lee still loved him. They then responded to Lee and wrote her a reply letter.

"Hi friend, this message is from Group Eight. Your letter was received and as you wished, we all read it together. The mail carrier gave us the letter while we were having lunch at the Cafeteria and we immediately opened it. We are sorry about your mother, Lee, we hope you are coping and we know you are a strong woman who can handle the situation. We are doing fine but you know the group is not complete without you and Popla. May God bless you to fulfil your dreams as a fashion designer one day and marry a man of your dreams, Bongani. We still sneak out to Mzala and go to Pretoria every fortnight to watch movies. You will forever be in our hearts, Lee, we love you. See you soon, goodbye."

The group didn't receive a letter from Popla and they could not send her a letter because they did not have her postal address. They convinced themselves that one day they would receive her letter or meet somehow.

Sky and the band continue to play at Mzala and the group always gave them support. People frequently visiting the tavern gave Sky the name, 'Motherland Queen.' The name stuck, but people also still called her Sky. Many people thought Sky was her government name and 'Motherland Queen' was a street name.

In the spring of 1996 people celebrated Spring Day to welcome spring. They played with water balloons to celebrate the end of winter, and they gathered in parks and in Mzala to listen to music. One Sunday, Sky and the band were entertaining people at Mzala, and they chose to play a new song Sky had written. The song was difficult to master, but they took a chance and played it. Their style of performing was nonstop triple play; in between, when Sky or a lead singer was preparing to come in with another song, KB and Segopotso continued playing their instruments to introduce the new song smoothly. The song was the last they were playing that day, and it was called 'Love Formula'.

I was just walking down Van der Walt street
never thought I can feel so miserable today
he looked at me and I pretended not to see him
he looked away but deep in my heart I wannet him
    to look again
when he look at me again
I looked back at him
he ask my name
I looked at the robot without a response but deep
    inside I wannet him to ask again
he ask my name again
I told him my name
not knowing you will disappear one day

(Chorus)
what is a love formula
seems like mine is wrong
what is a love formula
or am I calculating wrong (3x)
wish I never looked back when you looked at me
they say time heals
but my heart is cut into pieces
if time really heals
it will take a million years to heal
at night my dreams were shattered
I thought you were going to be my baby's father
you disappeared like a needle in a haystack
you disappeared without a reason
I heard you have another woman
what is her love formula
I want to use it one day
maybe mine is wrong
(Chorus)
what is a love formula
seems like mine is wrong
what is a love formula
or am I calculating wrong (3x)

Sky's friends were minding their own business, enjoying themselves and socialising with other people. When Sky started to sing the new song, her friends stopped what they were doing and, together with everyone else in the tavern, focused on her. After the song, Sky joined her friends at the table in the VIP area, together with Queen and the band. A white man was sitting alone, not far from their table, stood up and walked to their table. It was unusual for a white man to visit Mzala, especially a rough rural area like Siyabuswa which was famous for the riots in the eighties, called '*Mbhokotho*' – a battle between Sepedi- and Ndebele-speaking people.

The man introduced himself to Sky and everyone at the table. "Hi, my name is Hunter Dion from Dion Records." He held out his hand to shake hands with Sky. She accepted his hand with a charming smile and introduced him like a musician would after hearing that the man was from a recording company. "Sky, Motherland Queen, and these are my friends." He invited Sky to his table for a few drinks and her friends did not have a problem as they knew Sky could handle herself. It was also ok with her boyfriend. He knew Sky was faithful to him, and he also knew that the man from the recording company was there to talk about music.

The man ordered two whiskies, not knowing that Sky didn't drink alcohol, but before the waiter could deliver, she cancelled one whisky and ordered a juice. Without wasting time, Mr Dion explained why he had invited Sky to his table. He wanted to offer Sky a recording deal with Dion Records, but it did not include the band. He offered Sky a package that included ten thousand rand upfront, and a house and car immediately after she signed the contract, which would be for three years. Before Sky responded, she was curious to know who sent him because it was obvious that Hunter Dion was a first-time visitor to Mzala. People who visit Mzala often knew each other and a new visitor would be noticed immediately. The man pointed to Vincent Mo'Russia behind the bar counter. "He is an old friend of mine," he said. Vincent Mo'Russia was smiling behind the counter, but he didn't come to the table or make contact with Mr Dion until he left. It was as if they didn't want people to see them together. It was early years in South Africa's democracy and many people had big secrets about the apartheid era. Mr Hunter Dion just said he never explained how he became friends with Vincent Mo'Russia, or how or where they met.

Sky stood up and walked over to Vincent Mo'Russia and checked with him if he did know Mr Hunter Dion. He said he did, and that Sky need not be afraid, he had organised the deal. Sky must take the offer and not worry about the band, which would continue to play at Mzala.

"You deserve this, Sky, take the offer," he advised and patted Sky on the shoulder before turning and walking away. Sky was confused. She didn't know what to do or say. She looked over to where her friends were sitting with the band, and walked back to where Mr Dion was sitting and accepted the offer without any doubts – she trusted Vincent Mo'Russia. After all, he had given her the opportunity to show off her talent.

Sky accepted the offer without talking to her friends or the band; she believed it was her decision alone. Mr Dion invited her to come to Dion Records the following week to sign her contract. He stood up and gave her his business card before disappearing in the crowd.

Sky walked back to her friends and smiled. She was happy to have a recording deal. She told her friends about it and they were happy for her, but the band wasn't. They felt betrayed by Sky for accepting the recording deal and excluding them when they had been playing together for so long. Itumeleng and the others argued that Sky was not part of the band and had a right to sign a recording deal solo, after all Sky was the one writing the songs and coming up with the beats.

Heated words were exchanged until Vincent Mo'Russia came across to their table and ended the argument by telling the band to quit blaming Sky and that he would let them continue to play. He also offered to be the band's manager and promised to pay them double what he was paying Sky every month. That ended the argument and everyone was happy for Sky, congratulating her on the start of her new journey to becoming a professional musician.

Her next problem was to tell her parents about the recording deal.

The following week, Sky took a taxi to Dion Records situated in Sunnyside in Pretoria, ten minutes from the city centre. She didn't have a problem finding the place because she was now used to Pretoria, and knew the streets in the city centre and surrounding suburbs. Hunter Dion was waiting outside the building for Sky, smoking a cigar.

"Good morning Mr Dion," Sky greeted him with a big smile on her excited face.

"Hello Sky," he responded. "Please call me Hunter. The producer is dying to meet you. Come inside." They walked in and went first to Hunter's office where he gave Sky the contract to read. "Read it and then sign here when you are done, or ask questions if you don't understand something." He offered her tea or coffee, but Sky was too excited to have anything to drink. She just wanted to sign the deal.

There were many pages to read. On the cover page

were the words, 'Dion Records,' and the company logo. She took up the pen and signed the contract. Hunter then walked Sky to the studio. She had never seen a recording studio before and it was a thrilling experience. There was a large machine with many buttons, and a big glass cubicle with microphones. All she could say was, "Wow!" and walk around, looking more closely at all the equipment.

Hunter introduced her to Peter Masondo, who was known in the recording world as 'Blaza' – he was from Mamelodi West. He was a humble and patient person to work with when you were dropping an album. Sky asked to go inside the glass cubicle. Peter said it was ok, and she walked in and put on the headphones to try them out. She almost cried with excitement. Hunter pressed a button from outside and Sky heard his voice saying, "Come out for now, soon you will be in there every day, girl." As it was towards the end of year, Hunter told Sky to focus on her studies and then after writing exams, she must come to see her new house, her car, and she would be paid the ten thousand rand as stated in the contract.

This was all good new and Sky felt that God was opening a new door of her life. She finished writing her exams and she waited for her results before she went back to Hunter. It was scary for final-year students at Kwandebele College waiting to hear their results; a fail meant they would have to go to Nelspruit where the college had been incorporated into the University of Mpumalanga. Most of the students did not want to go that far from home.

The results were finally released after two long weeks, by which time, Hunter was starting to panic, thinking Sky changed her mind, but he kept his cool. Students were being given their results in the college reception area and some were crying when they opened their results, some were scared, and some were happy. Sky and her friends were standing in line waiting to collect their results – the rule was not to open your results until everyone had their results, and then they would open together in the park, chilling under a tree.

As they readied to open the envelopes, Itumeleng said, "Remember, whatever happens, it is not the end, ok?" Everyone passed. Sky again passed with high marks, followed by Lala, then Itumeleng, Bongani, Small and Joman. They had all made it through college and were going to graduate; thank God no one was going to Nelspruit or had to look for another college option.

CHAPTER 8
THE RECORDING ARTIST

Bongani found a job immediately in Limpopo as legal adviser at Hendry Mine in Northam; Itumeleng was appointed to be a manager at his father's driving school, Lala got a job as teacher at Moutse Primary School, Joman found a job back home in Burgersfort at Chrome Mine as a driller, and Small found a job at Thembisile Hani Municipality driving a grader. Small and Itumeleng saw each other often as they stayed in the same *kasi*. Itumeleng was also helping Small get a grader licence through his father's connections in Pretoria.

Sky was pursuing a career in music, but it was still a secret to her parents. Weeks after receiving her results, she told her parents that she a job as a teacher at a private school in Pretoria, and she tipped off Lala not to say anything about the record deal. Lala promised that her secret was safe with her – just as they had at college, they still protected each other.

The next day Sky kissed her parents goodbye, she said goodbye to Lala, and she went through to Pretoria to meet

Hunter, as promised. She met him at Dion Records, and then they went together to Waterkloof, an upper-class suburb on the eastern side of Pretoria, where the residents were predominantly white. They arrived at the gates of a large double-storey house and Hunter gave Sky the gate remote and said, "Sky, open the gate to your house."

She was overjoyed and couldn't believe it was indeed her home. She asked Hunter to repeat what he said about it being her house. Hunter laughed and confirmed that it was hers. They drove inside and parked in front of the double garage doors. Sky had no fear of Hunter because he was a friend of Vincent Mo'Russia – and nobody messes with Vincent Mo'Russia. She trusted him completely. In the time that she had played at Mzala, Vincent Mo'Russia had become more than an employer to her; he was a father figure and a friend. He always encour-aged Sky to study hard if she wanted to pursue a career in music.

They parked and walked to the sliding door at the front of the house, which Hunter opened. He showed her the whole house that had been furnished throughout with beautiful Italian furniture. At the back was a swimming pool surrounded by trees, roses, and citrus trees. They walked to the garage where a 1996 red BMW M3 dolphin, Bavarian Cabriolet 'abashwe' was parked. Hunter turned on the ignition and opened the roof top. He said, "This is the good life, Sky. I want you to be a millionaire." Sky could not believe this was her house and her car, but it was. Hunter handed over the house keys, the tittle deed, the car keys and the vehicle licence. The house and the car were in her name, and Hunter had organised a woman to help Sky get her driver's licence. He told her to relax and that they would start work in the studio in two weeks' time.

Sky enjoyed staying in her house for the first time, and every day in those two weeks, a woman arrived from Lubbe Driving School to take Sky for driving lessons. After a week and two days, the driving school instructor took Sky to a testing centre for her driver's licence, which she passed.

Hunter also came around and presented her with a cheque for ten thousand rand, as agreed in the contract, and told her she needed to be at the studio to start recording her first album the following Monday. He didn't have doubts because Vincent Mo'Russia had told him that Sky had been playing at Mzala for a long time, and that she was a good songwriter, who was also quick.

Sky did not want her first album to be old songs she had played at college or Mzala, so she wrote new songs for her first album over one weekend; it was a busy weekend without sleep, but it was also surprising because she wrote hip hop songs. The nineties was a decade of hip hop swag people listening to American rappers, but most of the young stars who got recording deals wanted to record hip hop.

On that Monday she got into her 'Bima', opened the roof top, and drove to the studio. Even though she was not a great driver, who was going to hoot at a Bima M3 Bavaria or shout rudely at the beautiful girl driving it! It was the nineties, and a woman driving a fancy car was classed as educated and rich. It was rare to see a woman driving a vehicle in that class.

In the basement parking lot was a parking bay labelled, 'Sky' in big letters on the wall. She parked and went upstairs where she found Blaza waiting. Hunter was out on business, but Blaza showed her the rehearsal room which had everything Sky would need. There was a microphone connected to speakers to connect her guitar, a white couch to rest on, a desk and chair to write or change her songs, and a bottle of water for refreshment. Sky was excited to see all the equipment – it felt like her office because it had everything she needed.

Sky had written ten songs for the album, which she titled, *Motherland Queen*, and included hits like 'Blue Train' and 'Sky Ville' and other songs that people loved.

Dion Records was a fairly new studio that had not yet had musicians who sold gold or platinum albums; most were just selling locally. After Sky's rehearsal, she took a break and then went into the studio. Blaza did not want her to feel too much pressure so he suggested she start the next day, but Sky was stubborn and she wanted to start immediately. She went into the cubicle, put on the head-phones, and gave Blaza a thumbs up to show she was ready. He smiled, pressed a button and she heard his voice in the headphones saying, "When the green light is on you can start, Sky."

He noticed that Sky did not have her guitar with her and he waited to see what she had in mind – he had decided to let her be free to do whatever she wanted. The green light came on and Sky started to sing. Blaza could not believe his ears. She wasn't singing country or Afropop, but it was incredible. The agreement was that she would sing Afro pop or country, but Blaza could hear that this was going to be a best-selling album. She was singing 'Sky Ville'.

Sky Ville oh yes my land
I rule I'm the queen so what
when I say jump you say how high
but I am the sweetest thing
I love I'm a lover that's who I am
I'm the new kid on the block
(Chorus)
I do my thing baby I do
I do my thing I do (4x)

It was the best song Blaza had heard since he started producing at Dion Records. Sky also recorded a voice that could be heard in the background when she was rapping.

'Uuh … yeah … you are baby... Uuh! … You are …'

Blaza put the song together with heavy bass in the background that complemented Sky's lyrics and he balanced it with treble sounds. Blaza phoned Hunter to come listen to Sky's single immediately – he couldn't wait for him to come back. When Hunter arrived, he agreed that indeed, the single was a hit. He also encouraged Sky to change from her old style of music to rap – hip hop was a booming genre of the nineties.

They continued to work on the project for three weeks and then Sky went to a photo shoot for the album cover. There she met a famous musician, Boy Max, who was also with Dion Records and was also there for a photo shoot for the cover of his album, *Baby Girl*, that was going to be released at the same time as *Motherland Queen*. Sky was excited to meet someone she had only previously seen on television. Boy Max was a big gun in the music industry. He started singing in 1992 and had a record deal with

Lewis Carl Records, but he left to join Dion Records after conflict with his manager. He recorded songs like, 'Heavenly Father' that gained him popularity, but didn't sell many copies.

Boy Max's full names were Maxwell Hlanjwa. He had grown up in Kwetyana near East London in the Eastern Cape and had moved to Johannesburg with his family in the eighties, to live in Jabavu in Soweto, where he had fallen in love with music. The popular music culture in Soweto was Kwaito, but he chose to sing R&B, influenced by American singers.

Boy Max fell in love with Sky immediately they met for their photo shoots, but Sky was not interested in him. He was eleven years older than her, he was not so charming, and he had a big beard and stretched long hair. Sky was still in love with Itumeleng even though they had been far apart from each other since their college days.

Motherland Queen was soon heard all over radio stations in South Africa, and 50 000 copies were sold within the first seventy-two hours following the release. Hunter was very happy with the sales, and on the day the album hit 50 000, he threw a party at Dion Records to celebrate where Sky was the star of the day, and she had the opportunity to meet other musicians recording under the Dion Records label.

Motherland Queen reached platinum in two weeks and was a major boost for Dion Records. Radio stations, newspapers, television channels, magazines from all over the world wanted to know who this girl, Sky, was. At the same time, Sky's parents were amazed to hear people talking about their daughter as a music star and to hear radio hosts discussing the album. Lala then confessed to Sky's parents that Sky was a musician, she had played at Mzala, and that she was not working as a teacher in a private school in Pretoria.

Motherland Queen was winning awards, locally and internationally, and the first time Sefako and Baby saw Sky since she had left home was on television accepting an award – she was wearing red leather trousers and a tight red top, and was as beautiful as her mother. Her parents had mixed feelings. They were happy for her, but also angry that their Lucky had lied to them. Lala told them that Sky had always loved music and had not wanted to disappoint them. She said they should be happy for Sky who had finished her studies to honour their wishes, she had passed with flying colours, and had then been given an opportunity to have a career in music.

Hunter was working hard – everyone wanted to interview Sky and he juggled the bookings for local and international media, and was also organising a video shoot. In the meantime, Sky was performing locally, rehearsing in the week and performing on weekends, from Friday to Sunday. She travelled all over South Africa, performing and doing interviews.

Sky's first interview had been on a national radio station called South FM, in the Midday Flight programme hosted by Charlie Mangers. The show had four million listeners, who heard how Sky had grown up in a rural area, raised as a single child by both parents, she had started writing songs and singing in primary school, how she attended college and sang at Mzala, and how Hunter Dion had been introduced to her and had given her a contract with Dion Records. Charlie Mangers was known to be a host who didn't leave any questions unasked. He asked Sky who her role models were – most people thought role models were famous people, leaders and celebrities. But Sky answered Charlie with a soft voice. "They are my parents, my father Sefako Molapo, and my mother, Baby Molapo. They raised me in the best possible way. They gave me the best education possible, but I chose a career in music. If you are listening, Father and Mother, please forgive me – music is in my heart." By then Sky was crying. Sefako and Baby were listening because Lala had told them she would be interviewed by Charlie Mangers, and they were deeply moved by her words.

Soon Sky was on all the front pages and on radio and television all over the world. Many musicians wanted to feature Sky in their projects, and a filmmaker was negotiating to use her in their movies.

After the winter of 1997, Hunter organised video shoots in Cape Town and Mauritius for the whole *Motherland Queen* album. Before Sky set off for those shoots, she took a two-week break to see her parents. It had been months since Sky had left home and she had missed her parents, but she wondered how they would react after seeing her face all over the media. She also missed Lala and could not wait to take her for a ride in the Bima and she also hoped to find out where Itumeleng was. She had lost contact with him because they had agreed to meet at midday on Saturdays at the Nelson Mandela statue at the Union Buildings, but Sky had been too busy with her projects to make those meetings.

It was on a Sunday and Sky was driving home to Mak

ville, not knowing that Hunter had contacted Vincent Mo'Russia to organise a big reception for Sky when she arrived home. The plan was to organise the Mak ville community to line the road and cheer her as a child of Mak ville who had made her community proud when she arrived. Hunter believed that would help to make sure that her parents realised how people loved their daughter for her music and they would not try to persuade her to give up her music. He didn't want to lose Sky from Dion Records.

Immediately after passing the filling station about eight hundred metres from Mak ville, Sky saw a crowd on the side of the road as she approached, screaming and praising her name, and shouting out her song, 'Back Home' which was on the *Motherland Queen* album and had fast become Mak ville's anthem among the young people. Kids were singing the song everywhere, and the adults knew it was a song composed and sung by their own Lucky Atlega Sky Molapo.

When Sky arrived home, her parents were very happy to see their daughter and Lala was happy to reunite with her friend. They were surprised to see Sky driving a car, and not just any car, but a top of the range BMW. Sky had also bought cell phones for her parents so that she could communicate with them when she was not around as she was spending a lot of time on the road.

For the whole two weeks, she drove her parents every-where – to the shops, visiting friends, and buy building material to build a new home for her parents. Sky was also bonding with Lala, they went to different places, chilled, and Sky told Lala about her life in Pretoria and about the famous people she had met. Lala also updated Sky on changes in Mak ville, her job as a teacher, and that she was still with Joman, who often visited her in Mak ville.

They also visited Vincent Mo'Russia and the band she used to play with at Mzala, to catch up on each other's news and to socialise. The people of Mak ville and the surrounds loved seeing the two beautiful girls in the Bima with the top down, driving around their area. Parents began encouraging their children to work hard to succeed, giving Sky as the example of what they could achieve.

On the Saturday evening at the end of her two weeks at home, Sky went into the living room to sit on the couch with her parents. She apologised about everything. She looked them in the eyes, cried, and asked for their blessing on her career in the music industry. This was the first time Sefako and Baby had heard their daughter telling them about her love for music, and they were glad she was doing something she loved. They also apologised to her for putting so much pressure on her to be a teacher. She heard then that it had been her mother's childhood dream to be a teacher, but her parents could not afford to send her to college, and instead they arranged for her to marry Sefako, who had turned out to be the love of her life. Her parents loved each other deeply and had raised her to be a strong woman.

After the serious talk, she told her parents about the upcoming trip to Cape Town and Mauritius for video shoots the following week, and they were very excited that their daughter was going abroad for the first time. She kissed her parents goodbye, and as usual, Lala was also there to say goodbye to her friend.

As Sky reversed her Bima, her mother said, "Never forget where you come from my child, you were raised by Makometsane, but we understand that the world also needs you," and she blew kisses to Sky as she drove away. Sefako was sad to see his daughter leave, but he was happy that she had become a young lioness. Before she left he had said to her, "Don't take long to come home again, my child." Lala also blew kisses to her friend; she was proud to have a friend like Sky, and she promised to give Itumeleng Sky's contact details if they met up by chance.

Sky drove back to her home in Pretoria, and the following Tuesday, she went to Dion Records to meet up with Hunter, who was pleased to see her, and told her that the big reception in Mak ville had been his idea to convince her parents that she belonged in the music industry.

Hunter then briefed her on the trip, which would be from Tuesday 9 September to Friday 10 October 1997. Hunter had alerted the media about her trip, as well as the airport and the police, for protection. He had also found sponsors who would pay for the whole trip, video shoots, and for a fashion designer. Sky was excited to hear that she could also use the designer for her private purposes, to not more than six thousand rand. The sponsor would also give her a monthly allowance of two thousand rand for petrol until the end of her contract with Dion Records.

On 9 September, a car came to collect her and drive her to Johannesburg International Airport, where she found Hunter waiting with the dance troupe. He had organised her passport and visa and all the bookings as she had no experience of international travel at that stage. It was indeed a big day for her; she was going to fly for the first time, which was scary, but she was also excited to be living her dream.

Airport workers, members of the media, and a crowd of fans had gathered to see the girl that everyone was talking about. She walked with Hunter and the rest of the crew to the check-in counters, escorted by police to protect her from the crush of the crowds, the media and the cameras.

The crew walked behind with all the bags and Hunter walked in front with the police, opening a path for her to pass through and make sure no one got too close. The woman at the check-in counter was thrilled to be serving Sky – she tried to stay calm, but she was shaking with excitement and stamped the passport without checking the documentation.

They then walked to a section set aside for short media interviews, before it was time for them to board the flight to Cape Town. They were escorted onto the plane, where Hunter and Sky were settled into their first-class seats. Sky was looking a bit scared and Hunter turned to her and said, "Everything will be ok, Madam." He was chuckling. He had started calling her 'Madam' when she became a top-selling and award-winning artist. Dion Records had grown a lot in the few months since Sky's album had been released. Sky was also on her way to becoming the first young black woman artist millionaire in South Africa, and it was estimated that after her video shoots, her net worth would double.

It was Hunter's idea that after the video shoots, Sky should come up with another hit album. They checked in to the Sun Rise Hotel in Cape Town's centre city by three o'clock in the afternoon, and decided that they would rest and gather the next day at midday in the hotel lobby to finalise the day's shoot with the camera crew.

Sky took a walk with her makeup artist Betty 'Ginger' Kruger outside the hotel to see the sights, and the women were awed at how beautiful the city was. Around the hotel were rose bushes in bloom, closer to the beach they could hear the waves on the rocks, and Table Mountain loomed over the city, majestic and magnificent. Back inside the hotel reception, Sky was amazed at how bright it was.

Her room was furnished all in white. Her king-sized bed was covered in white linen, the curtains in front of the blackout screens were white, and the bathroom was a study in white from wall to wall. Ginger had come into her room with her, and Sky said, "Ginger, this is like a place where angels live!" They laughed and went to the window to look at the view of the ocean, with boats bobbing on the waves and the horizon stretching into the far distance. Ginger responded, "We are angels, darling!"

Everything was cool, and even her experience of room service was excellent, except that she was persuaded to eat seafood for the first time by Ginger, who wanted her to try something different. At first Sky looked at the prawns, looked at Ginger, and said, "How can I eat this thing with so many legs, Ginger?" The only thing that looked familiar was the fish; everything else was a new experience. Ginger was laughing, but she showed Sky how to eat the prawns, and from that day, she fell in love with seafood.

Sky and the crew did four successful music video shoots, one at Sea Point and three on Clifton Beach. The managers of the hotel asked Hunter to shoot some of Sky's music video in the hotel reception for a seventy per cent discount to promote the hotel. Everyone loved the look of the hotel, especially the reception area which was beautifully welcoming, and they agreed to the offer.

They were in Cape Town for about two weeks and then flew to Mauritius for remaining three music videos. They were staying at the Blue Roof Hotel, which was close to Blue Bay Beach where the shooting was going to take place. It was a beautiful hotel, decorated in a modern style. The name, Blue Roof, came from hotel roofs that had all been painted bright blue. The rest of the hotel was white, like Sun Rise Hotel, and it was also beautiful inside and outside, with a lovely view of the ocean from the rooms. Standing on the balcony on the ocean side, you could see waves crashing onto the beach and then going back into the ocean.

The shooting of the *Motherland Queen* music videos for 'Sky Ville' and 'Back Home' was done at Blue Bay Beach in the Souillac area and Gris Gris Beach. The media was already classing the music videos as among the best and most expensive yet seen in the South African music industry.

Hunter organised a party at the Blue Roof Hotel to celebrate when the shooting was done, and later the party moved to the hotel bar. Sky felt as if she was on top of the world, following the successful shooting of the entire *Motherland Queen* album. Later the party moved from the rooftop to the bar, where people saw Sky drinking alcohol for the first time. Usually she just had juice to drink. She was sitting at a table with Hunter drinking red wine – and at about midnight, she simply vanished. The next day, Ginger went to Sky's room, and found Sky feeling sick, throwing up, and not remembering what had happened the night before. Ginger told her she had a hangover and ordered her food and cold water to drink.

Sky told Ginger that even though she couldn't remember much of the previous evening, she did remember that she had felt good.

They all returned to South Africa and the music videos were an instant and massive hit – they were playing on television stations around the world, and were selling like crazy. Sky's net worth was growing, and Dion Records became the most sought-after record label for musicians across the country – Hunter became the 'Pretoria Godfather'.

Back home, Ginger and Sky were good friends, sharing stories about their lives, chatting about boys, and spending a lot of time together at Sky's home. One morning they walked to the nearby filling station to buy bread and people gaped at them wherever they went, which was not surprising. In the shop, they noticed a newspaper with a picture of Sky and Hunter on the front page, under the headline, 'Music star dates her boss'. They didn't even buy the bread they were there for because Sky was so angry. They went home and Sky phoned Hunter to tell him about the newspaper article. He said he had seen it. He had been in the music industry for a long time and was used to media rumours – he answered Sky, "Welcome to the music industry."

Ginger, however, remembered the day Sky had vanished from the bar in Mauritius when she had been sitting and drinking wine with Hunter, and then she had vanished at about midnight. Ginger asked Sky about that night, but Sky swore nothing had happened. She said Hunter had taken her up to her hotel room, before leaving for his room. Ginger asked more questions because Sky had not remembered what had happened the night before when Ginger went to her room in the morning, when Ginger realised she wasn't getting anywhere with her questions, she stopped asking.

The next story to break in the media was the rumour that said Sky was a drunkard, and very soon, negative stories about Sky were being carried in the media everywhere. Sky maintained her story that she was not dating Hunter, and whenever another negative story was published, she would say, "Freedom comes if you let things go away." They were strong words that made people believe she was a strong woman.

Sefako and Baby were worried about the negative stories about Sky, particularly that she was drinking alcohol. It was also hard for Lala to see the stories because often when stories were carried about celebrities taking drugs, they proved true in the end.

That year Sky spent Christmas with her parents and Lala at her house in Waterkloof, and spent the holidays trying to forget about the music industry. Sky bought Christmas gifts for them all – a watch for her father, a beautiful necklace for her mother, and to Lala she gave a diary with naughty stuff from college. It was lovely to spend the festive season with family, who were also celebrating the completion of the new house Sky had built for her parents. The house was double-storey with eighteen rooms and two garages. The walls were painted grey and the gate was painted black. It was the only double-storey in Mak ville, and it could be seen from quite a distance when entering the village.

The day after Christmas Lala went out to throw some garbage in the waste bin, using the door into the garage. In the corner in front of Sky's Bima, she saw a recycling bin, in which were many empty wine bottles. Lala realised that the media was not lying about her friend's drinking, but she didn't say anything because she didn't want to ruin Christmas.

CHAPTER 9
THE WEALTHY MUSIC STAR

In January 1998, Dion Records was again celebrating *Motherland Queen*, which had won another prestigious award as the best album of 1997. Sky won the 'best hip hop female singer' and 'best songwriter' of 1997.

One day she was in the studio, working on her new album called *Good Morning*, when the receptionist came to tell her that someone – a tall handsome man – was in reception, asking for her. Sky took a break and walked with the receptionist to the reception area. To her amazement, the person was Itumeleng. She ran to him and jumped into his arms – they greeted each other happily, and Sky told the receptionist to tell Blaza she was going out for a few minutes.

They went to the coffee shop across the road from Dion Records, and they ordered coffee and muffins. When the order arrived, even though Itumeleng was left-handed, he was keeping his left hand hidden. He then said, "I love you Sky, but there is something I have to tell you and it is not good news." He looked so sad that Sky was alarmed.

"What is it Itumeleng?" He took out his left hand and showed her. On his second finger he was wearing a ring. Sky looked at him then back at a ring and tears started falling. Itumeleng told her he was married and had a six-month-old child, and that they were living in Groblersdal. He said that while he was working at his father's driving school, one day he was helping a white guy get his licence when, in their conversation, he found out that the man had a law firm. He hired Itumeleng, which is where he met a nice girl, Sheron Mmamadisa from the Tafelkop area, who was working as the manager of a clothing store, near the law firm.

They met daily at a fast-food outlet and then they started dating. They were married in a traditional wedding, and when the child was born, she was named Lucky Manaka Mmamadisa after Sky. They had both agreed on the name, although Sheron thought it was chosen because Lucky was a famous musician; she didn't know that Lucky had been Itumeleng's lover in college.

Sky was very sad to hear the news, but she accepted that it had been her own fault because she had focused on her music career and had not given Itumeleng a chance after college, and she had not made much of an effort to find him. Instead of getting angry, she apologised to Itumeleng for letting him down and giving up on their relationship. He had waited for Sky, thinking she would come back to him, but he gave up when the media started publishing all the negative stories about Sky. He thought she was living the high life and had forgotten about him.

They both accepted that they were now living in different worlds. After the coffee break, it was time for

Itumeleng to return home but Sky begged him to stay for a night. It was hard for him to refuse because he still loved her, and no man could say no to Motherland Queen. The problem was what was he going to tell his wife. Together they came up with a plan to say that his vehicle had broken down on the R573 in the middle of nowhere and he had to sleep in the car, waiting for someone to come and rescue him. In the nineties, not many people could afford cars so there were not many on the road. Sky told Blaza that one of her cousins was in town and she needed to take him to his place, and she would continue with the project the next day. Blaza knew the project was ahead of schedule and didn't have a problem with Sky leaving early.

Itumeleng was following Sky's Bima in his Cressida GLI 6 to Waterkloof, deeply regretting that he had married Sheron and left Sky. Her success and the car she was driving amazed him. When they arrived at her place, he felt happy for Sky, but he wasn't happy with the decision he had made.

Sky opened the gate and drove in, followed by Itumeleng. They walked to the front door with Itumeleng walking behind Sky and watching her behind. Oh! Sky was so beautiful. She had a nice body was blessed with bumps and curves in all the right places. Most men looked back at her when they passed Sky, to take in her beauty.

Inside, they went to the lounge and she invited Itumeleng to a seat on the couch, and then offered him wine, water, coffee, or juice. He laughed and chose whisky. It was a surprise that Itumeleng had chosen whisky as none of the Group Eight had taken alcohol in college.

Later that afternoon, Sky was cooking and sipping

wine, and Itumeleng sat on the other side of the kitchen, sipping whisky, chopping vegetables, and chatting about the past.

After dinner, Sky prepared a bath for Itumeleng, and once he had been in for a few seconds, she came into the bathroom naked. Chubby thighs, birthmark next to her belly button, small pink lips parted, she stood and looked at Itumeleng. He was shy and looked at her and then down at the bath, he was smiling. Sky climbed into the bath and settled down between Itumeleng's legs, leaning back on his chest. She started murmuring in a low voice, "Just imagine you and I naked for the first time, you should have waited. Just imagine you and I married with lot of kids in the house calling me Mom and you Daddy. Why did you not wait? I was focusing more on papers, forgetting life is not about papers but being happy. Yes money makes you happy, but it does not buy you a family. Why did you not wait for me? You should not have given up on our love, you should have known better the way I loved you ... but I don't blame you, I blame the papers of happiness."

She turned her head to look at Itumeleng in the eyes, then her face drew closer and closer to Itumeleng's face as if she was hypnotising him, until their lips touched. They kissed and touched as in a Hollywood movie, and then she was screaming Itumeleng's name, slowly, breaking it up into three syllables.

That night her bedroom was so busy that anyone passing her bedroom door would have thought world war three was happening inside. In the morning she was tired but happy, and then it was time for Itumeleng to leave; his wife was waiting and could not sleep because her husband had not come home the night before. As he was reversing his car, Sky went to his window and said, "I don't care if you are married, I will wait for you. Don't take long." Itumeleng smiled and promised to come back, but his heart was no longer with Sky, he was already practising the explanation he was going to give his wife.

Sky then had to prepare to go into the studio to finish the *Good Morning* project. When she arrived, Blaza was waiting for her. To his surprise, Sky went straight into the cubicle and started to sing a song she later named, 'It hurts but...' about a woman who was hurt by someone she loved.

It hurts when you love someone
always waiting but never shows up
later hear he has a wife
surprised, then you hear he got a child
he was a man of my dreams
at college he was my friend
and he was my bae
I loved him he loved me
my first boyfriend
my first love I missed you
oh! I do not blame him
I was always busy taming the big fives
I want them to run around my field
my pockets filled with wild animals
I didn't care about the ones I loved the most
it was about money
just imagine you and I naked for the first time
you should have waited

Imagine you and I married
lot of kids in the house calling me Mom and you
     Daddy
Why didn't you wait?
I was focusing more on papers
forgetting life is not about papers but about being
     happy
yes money makes you happy
but does not buy you a family
why didn't you wait?
you should not have given up on our love
you should have known better the way I loved you
but I don't blame you
I blame the papers of happiness
(Continue)

Sky was rapping nonstop and when Blaza put the song together it played for ten minutes. It was the longest song of nineties, and it was a hit. Blaza and Hunter were not surprised to hear a song by Sky with sad lyrics – she wrote both happy and sad songs. Who cares, all they wanted was money and they believed money could make people happy.

Hunter and Blaza had given Sky that mentality, but then she had realised that money does not make people happy once she found out that Itumeleng was married. Sky did not want to be second in Itumeleng's life, but it was too late. He chose to stay a married man. She really loved Itumeleng, but she did not want the situation to derail her from her music, so instead, she decided to make herself feel better by writing songs about the situation. Her next song was called 'Ghetto Respect'.

I'm from the ghetto small ville Mak ville
this is where I learnt respect
Went to College at Motherland
this is where I was crowned Motherland Queen
I love my fans they put bread on my table
they love me back
Respect, people will respect you back
people will love you back
money can't buy love
money can't buy respect
can't force people to love you
can't force people to respect you
you earn it, that's ghetto respect
Then the song went into a strong beat that hit you
    deep in the core of your heart, with Sky's voice
    singing the chorus.
(Chorus)
Can't force people to love
can't force people to respect you ...
learn the ghetto life
is how you will learn to respect
is how you will learn to love

After the chorus, she started to rap and the song was a hit on the *Good Morning* album, which also included hit songs like 'Who That' which was released on Valentine's Day in 1998.

Hunter was organising a promotion of the album in the beautiful Pretoria Union Buildings park. The album sold platinum within seven days all over the world. It was soon popular in Europe, United States, Russia, Middle East, and

Africa, and in Africa, the most popular song was 'Forgotten World', especially in west and central Africa, because it talked about Africa.

> *We hear you speaking*
> *who represent us as Africans*
> *or we just add the number*
> *we don't have to say anything*
> *we just have to say yes to everything*
> *Africa need a voice Benin 'wanna' speak*
> *who represents CAR*
> *Burundi 'wanna' speak*
> *we love you Burkina*
> *we love you Mali*
> *Africa needs a voice*
> *Malawi 'wanna' speak*
> *who represents Gambia*
> *Zimbabwe 'wanna' speak*
> *we love you Lesotho*
> *we love you South Africa*
> *our leaders have to stand up*
> *we didn't send them to sit and listen*
> *they got our message please say something*
> *don't be quiet our children are starving*
> *Africa say …*
> *(Continue)*

After the release of *Good Morning*, her net worth rose to $18 million, and Sky was given an honorary doctorate by the University of the Witwatersrand for her inspiring music. Sky's assets included shares in gold and diamond mining. She was the first woman to own a national radio station, which was called SKY FM. She also owned a Cessna Citation Jet which she named Baby after her mother. The 'Sky' clothes label was launched in Cape Town's Hout Bay, and she also had shares in a game lodge the Magaliesberg area, a farm near Mak ville, restaurants in Sandton and Cape Town that were named Queen, and she established a foundation called SKYCF, Sky Care Foundation, which raised funds to help matriculants pass well to further their studies at universities of their choice. She wanted to help kids whose parents could not afford to pay college or university fees, motivated by Lala who was able to go to Kwandebele College through the help of funding by her father's employers.

Sky was in the top three richest women in South Africa, the number one richest black woman, and the number one youngest rich person in South Africa. She wanted to move her parents from Mak ville to wherever they wanted to go, but they refused to leave their community. Mak ville had raised their daughter to be a better person, and they always reminded her not to forget that home is where charity begins.

One Saturday, Sky was promoting her album at a concert in Pretoria's CBD, from four in the afternoon until the early hours of the morning. Local artists were performing first, and then Sky was going to come on stage from ten o'clock at night until one in the morning, which would be followed by local DJs continuing the music until morning.

The streets were packed with people from all over South Africa who came to see Sky promoting her new album. Streets surrounding the CBD were closed and the traffic police were on duty as they knew this concert would attract people from far and wide. Security was beefed up and the roads that were closed to traffic were used as parking lots.

The stage was built next to the High Court on Paul Kruger Street facing Bosman Station. Between the stage and Vermeulen Street was a tent accommodating VIPs, but Sky was a VVIP and the plan was that she would enter without people noticing, and go straight to the stage, and then leave immediately after performing. Sky was always accompanied by security when she performed, provided by Dion Bouncers, which provided protection for celebrities. It was a company owned by Hunter, and he had given Sky a twenty per cent shareholding as a thank you for what she had done for his recording company.

People still suspected that the two were dating secretly when they saw everything Hunter did for Sky, not realising that he only wanted her to stick with Dion Records. Hunter made Sky rich, but he soon realised she was independent and could leave at any time to start her own recording label. Sky was loyal – if you played an important role in her life she would honour you, unless you messed up. She hadn't thought of leaving Dion Records. Hunter had given her the opportunity to became a successful musician, and she always remembered the words Hunter said to her: "I will make you a millionaire." Hunter also noticed that artists who featured Sky on their albums at Dion Records also had their albums fly off the shelves.

Sky was escorted from Waterkloof by Dion Bouncers, driving her imported Chevrolet Suburban SUV that had left-hand steering, which was another gift from Hunter, for the platinum sales of her *Good Morning* album.

At ten o'clock, Sky was standing on stage, people were shouting, the screens were showing her throughout the CBD, which was packed to capacity. Her line up was 'Sky Ville', 'Motherland Queen', 'Blue Train', 'Ghetto Respect', 'Good Morning', 'So What', 'Mfanaka', 'Pretoria night', 'Love life', 'Games of Love', 'Forgotten World' and songs by other artists where she had been featured. The song that created chaos in Church Square, with people crying and fainting from excitement, was 'Good Morning'.

In the morning at six o' clock cars hooting,
ambulance and police with sirens, driving on the
*   fast lane*
is Monday people tired from the weekend
hangover ooh! Why you cut me off
Hey! Why you drive like a maniac
is Sky I'm late
I'm a hustle
I don't have a job like you
my Bima is changing lanes
left to right and right to left
My boy Blaza is waiting
damn we hungry
we need to drop a hit
we need to shake the world
and make them cry
chasing papers
we ate all the big fives now chasing Benjamins
I never imagined myself in a Chevy Suburban

a mention on a mountain
Facing the ocean
Sky on the balcony wearing all white
looking at the waves
hit the shores and go back meet the waves
my money
my cars
my house
my diamond ear rings
my gold chain
my farm
my jet
Fame
my everything
living above the clouds and no more colas
popping champagne and tasting wine
the sun has set
new day comes
yeah! Sky, Good morning

The song had seventy verses and no chorus, only Sky's voice humming in the background as she rapped, and it wasn't surprising that the album sold platinum in a short period. Ambulances on standby around the CBD were starting to help people who were fainting. Sky's new album promotion also benefitted the city as several hundred thousand people flocked into the city, and the tourism sector was boosted by millions within only twenty-four hours.

It was a show that stunned the world, and soon Sky was receiving invitations from world leaders, royalty, organisations, and wealthy people who wanted a private performance, or to raise funds for an organisation.

Sky was travelling the world and also making time to visit her family, but the thing that was not sitting well with her was that since college, she had never met up with Group Eight; the only people she saw often were Itumeleng, and Lala and her boyfriend, Joman. Writing letters had become a thing of the past; people were starting to afford cell phones, but even if the other members of Group Eight had cell phones, no one knew their contact details.

One day she visited Vincent Mo'Russia at Mzala. It was still the old tavern, but Queen and the band were no longer playing there. Vincent Mo'Russia told Sky that they had started stealing alcohol from the storeroom, and so he decided it was time they left Mzala. Sky was visiting him to say thank you – she gave Vincent Mo'Russia a cheque for thirty thousand rand to renovate Mzala, and free advertising on Sky FM. Sky wanted the tavern to grow because this was where she had first met her fans. She also wanted to say thank you to Vincent Mo'Russia because he had given Sky her first break.

He was happy to receive the thirty thousand rand, and happier to see that the young college girl who used to play at Mzala had become a big star. For Sky just to walk into Mzala, attracted crowds. People said that everything that Sky touched turned to gold. On the first weekend after she visited Mzala, it was packed more than ever before and was more popular than ever.

A few months after the release of *Good Morning*, Sky and the Dion Records crew went to locations around South Africa to do video shoots for the album. They went to a mango farm in Venda in Limpopo in the north-eastern corner of South Africa, to a banana farm near Sabie in Mpumalanga, to Mak ville's Moutse Nature Reserve, where they did a shoot for the song, 'Good Morning,' to Pretoria's Bosman Station, and to Zanzibar in Tanzania to do the video shoot for 'Forgotten World', which was best loved by various African countries.

Hunter decided to organise an African tour for Sky from South to West Africa, which became known as the Cross Nations Tour. The countries they would tour included Botswana, Lesotho, Burundi, Comoros, Djibouti, Cameroon, Chad, Gabon, Sao Tome, Benin, Mauritania, Togo, Senegal, Sierra Leon, Ivory Coast and Gambia. Hunter chose these countries because the world was not talking about them a lot, as if they didn't exist, and he believed that including them in a tour by Sky would make them more recognised by the world. It was a two-month tour to sixteen African countries, nonstop, starting from Botswana and ending in Gambia. The media thought it would be impossible to perform in sixteen countries in two months nonstop, and Sky was invited to interviews with many media platforms, but Hunter didn't allow any inter-views. He believed the media wanted to demoralise Sky, and he wanted to prove a point that it is possible to have a tour of that scope. If it was successful, it would be a world record.

Before the tour, Sky was playing around in the studio one breaktime, with four other artists who were with Dion Records, and they ended up recording a single she called, 'Be Happy Mama', featuring the four artists and herself. The artists were Leeu de Jager, an Afrikaans singer; Paul

James, a country music singer; Lenny Schoeman, a classic tenor singer; and a rapper, Sipho 'King' Mabuza.

Hunter and Blaza had been arguing with Sky and with Lenny, the classic tenor, that you cannot combine hip hop music with an orchestra, which was when Sky came up with the idea to prove it since they were in the studio. She wrote a song that accommodated all four artists in their style of music, then gave them their scripts to practise, before going into the recording cubicle to prove their point. The song start with classical singing by Lenny accompanied by a violin, before the beat started.

(Lenny)
haa! … Mama …
you raised me up to be a woman
I am proud to call you mama
huu! … Be happy mama …
(Leeu)
mama … ek Is lief vir jou
jy het my groot gemaak om 'n man te wees
ek maak nou my kinders groot soos jy my groot
    gemaak het
ek sien my kinders is gelukkig soos my kinderjare
jy het hierdie mens groot gemaak mama
elke vrou wens ek kan hallo se
jy het 'n koning groot gemaak, wees trots
wees trots dat jy dit gedoen het
wees gelukkig mama
(King)
I'm sorry for the pain
I'm sorry I was naughty

I'm sorry for the friends I chose
sorry
I'm sorry it was anger
my father wasn't there
I'm sorry for the bad thing I have done
Sorry I'm sorry
I'm sorry I didn't mean to be a thief
end up in prison and every month you came to visit
hate to see you cry
I learnt my lesson
I'm a changed man
believe me mama
Just be happy
uuh! I'm sorry
damn I messed up
(Paul)
looking back where I come from
taking drugs with my friends
coming home late after curfew
jumping the gate and get into my bedroom window
find you sitting on my bed crying and waiting for me
to come home
not knowing if I will come or it will be the police
but you were strong and never gave up
today I'm the man mama
you raised me up as a single parent and you did
be happy mama
(Sky)
it was tough, it was hard
it was love that made me
yes, you made it

Lucky I had a father on my side
raising me like man
my mother on the other side teach me how to be a
    woman
I am independent
I am the Queen
the Motherland Queen
now I am the Queen of the South
wait, now I am the Queen of Africa
wait, man I am the Queen of the world
all because of you mama
be happy

Blaza put the song together and then they all listened. In the middle of the song, Hunter looked at Blaza and whispered in his ear, "Damn the girl is good, Blaza." Hunter could not believe his eyes that Sky had managed to combine different types of music in one song, especially including Afrikaans and orchestral music. 'Be Happy Mama' was released as a single featuring Sky, Leeu, Lenny, Paul, and King, and copies flew off the shelves. The media was as surprised as Hunter to hear the song. No other artist had previously composed a song with such a mixture of artists and music genres.

In early August 1998, Sky began her tour in Gaborone in Botswana, accompanied by Hunter, Ginger, her makeup artist, and other artists signed with Dion Records who volunteered to be part of the Cross Nations Tour. This other artists touring with Sky knew they would benefit in promoting their own albums, and not all of them would be in the same place at the same time.

Hunter divided them into groups so that they could all have an equal chance to be on stage, but they all needed to be in Gambia for the close of the tour.

Neither Sky nor Dion Records had to pay a cent for the tour. Everything was paid for by sponsors – hotels, transport, stages, clothing, and security. The tour covered the fifteen countries by the end of September 1998 and the crew flew from Ivory Coast to Gambia to close the tour. Sky's Cessna Citation Jet, Baby, took off on Thursday, 1 October from Aboisso Airport in Abidjan in Ivory Coast to land at Banjul International Airport in Gambia. The closing of the tour was going to take place at Independence Stadium in Bakau to the west of Banjul on Sunday 4 October.

As Sky left Aboisso Airport, crowds were there to see her, reaching out to touch her, shouting her name, with tears flowing down their faces. It was chaos, and both airport security and the Cross Nations Tour security were overpowered by the people who wanted to see Sky in person. The security ended up escorting Sky to the VIP waiting room until it was time to board the jet because the situation had gotten out of hand. As Baby, the Cessna Citation jet took off, Sky looked out at the airport packed with people, and realised that the situation had not been safe.

Banjul International Airport was also packed with people when Baby the jet landed. Authorities had already beefed up security when they heard what had happened at Aboisso Airport. The jet door dropped down and the first to exit were four Dion Bouncers bodyguards, then Sky walked down the stairway, and then Hunter and six more bodyguards and the crew followed.

Cameras didn't flash and people didn't scream until Sky came out and the uproar started. It got worse when Sky waved at the waiting crowd. Sky sometimes dressed to show off her body, but most often, she wore simple and expensive clothes such as jeans and golf shirts. She was more beautiful dressed in simple clothes than in tight skirts or shorts, and that day at Banjul International Airport she was wearing jeans and a shirt with a gold chain with a dollar sign pendant, black diamond ear rings, a gold watch, a gold bracelet, and a dollar sign cap. Law enforcement from Banjul escorted her Chevy Suburban, which had arrived on a flight, to the Bakau Hotel, close to Independence Stadium where she was going to close the tour. The crew rested for two days after their busy nonstop fifteen country tour, which was being declared a success by the media.

Sky was tired and Hunter refused media interviews for her, but promised that she would be available for interviews after the tour, from 12 October. The media started to speculate that Hunter was being too controlling of Sky, others thought he was hiding something – maybe Sky had been forced to continue with the tour. Sky had always wanted to ignore the media unless it was something related to her music; she wasn't interested in rumours. Whenever Hunter told Sky the media wanted an interview, she always asked, "About what?" before deciding if she would do it or not.

The closing of the Cross Nations Tour was going to start at ten o'clock in the morning and go on until four o' clock in the afternoon. Sky was going to be on stage for thirty minutes from midday, giving local artists and other artists more time to show off their talent.

That morning she woke up and began preparing to go on stage. Ginger did her makeup and helped her choose the outfit she would wear on stage. At forty-five minutes to her performance, she was escorted from the Bakau Hotel by the security guards to the stadium in her Chevy Suburban, with Hunter and Ginger following. Outside the hotel people gathered to watch the motorcade of vehicles, including Gambian police with sirens blaring, leave with Sky and the crew. People had also gathered along the road to watch her go past − it was as if a presidential motorcade was passing.

At the entrance of the stadium, others were waiting for the motorcade to see Sky before she entered, and about five hundred metres from the gate, the motorcade slowed down, the window of the Chevy Suburban rolled down and Sky started waving at the crowds. They went wild, screaming and running after the vehicles while the security and police jumped out to stop them coming closer to Sky.

She climbed out of the car, shoes first. They were diamond-studded SKY label sneakers. She was wearing bucket jeans and a white t-shirt with the words, 'Death is the Limit' printed on the front, and about twenty gold necklaces. The clothes had been specially designed for Sky for the Cross Nations Tour and she wasn't going to wear them again.

She started with her first song, 'Be Happy Mama'. Lenny went on stage first, followed by Leeu, King and then Paul. When they reached the part where Sky came in, the stage was dark and at first only her voice was heard. Then they could see her on stage and on the screens, and they screamed and shouted, "Sky we love you!" over and over.

When Leeu, King and Paul had left the stage after the song, she came up with a phrase before she started the next song.

Who that, who that …
Sky!
who's in the Capital …
Sky!

As she sang, "Who that, who that", the crowd shouted Sky, and that became a tradition for her on stage.

Sky sang a few songs from her old album, *Motherland Queen*, and a few from *Good Morning* and then closed with 'Forgotten World'. Five minutes before her thirty minutes came to an end, the stadium collapsed on the north wing, and she was advised to stop the performance immediately. The stadium had a capacity of twenty-eight thousand, but that day it was over-crowded because the demand for tickets was so great.

Tragedy struck, and the collapse of a part of the stadium caused a stampede and four hundred people died that day, including children. The world was watching, but they didn't blame Sky, they blamed the people who allowed over-crowding in the stadium. SKYCF and Dion Records donated fifteen million rand to help compensate the families of the deceased, and another eight million rand to help the Gambian government repair the stadium. It was a day the world would not forget, especially in Gambia, and it was always remembered as Cross Nations Day in Gambia.

CHAPTER 10
GRIEVING NATION

Sky spent two weeks with her family and Lala at her Hout Bay home in Cape Town after the tour, to recover from the tragedy at Independence Stadium, and rest after the hectic Cross Nation Tour.

It was good to spend time with her parents until they started to question her about her love life. They had never met a boyfriend of hers, or heard Sky talking about boys. They were starting to ask questions like, when are we going to see a grandchild? When are we going to meet your boyfriend? When are you going to get married? The questions annoyed her and she would change the subject.

Lala too, was advising her how to balance a career and love life. Lala didn't think it was a good idea for Sky to continue dating Itumeleng as he was married, but Sky insisted, saying Itumeleng was her man from college. Sky was a successful independent and beautiful woman and men tended to be afraid of approaching a woman of that calibre. If you were not confident, there was no way you could approach Sky and say, "I love you."

When Sky returned to the studio, she found that Dion Records had signed a new hip hop artist, Sabina 'Makoma' Kgole from Limpopo. Sabina was also called Sabrina, and was the same generation as Sky. She was from Seshego Zone Two in the city of Pietersburg, and was the daughter of a pastor, Steven Kgole and Martha Kgole, who was a stay-at-home mother. Sabina had started singing in church, but she dropped out of school in standard nine to pursue her dream to be a musician. She had run away from home to Johannesburg, and had ended up living on the streets until she became a prostitute to pay for a flat in Hillbrow.

Sabrina was a singer part time at the Moonlight Club in Hillbrow, but she also hustled on the side, dealing drugs. She was once arrested at Johannesburg International Airport trying to smuggle drugs from South Africa to Europe, and she was sentenced to five years in prison. She was released early for good behaviour, and returned to Hillbrow and the Moonlight Club, but she stopped dealing drugs.

Hunter saw Sabrina performing at Moonlight Club and he offered her a five-year contract with Dion Records. Sabrina had written songs in prison, about her experiences in prison, and about her life in general, as well as love songs. Her first album with Dion Records was called *I am sorry* – she was apologising to her parents, and trying to explain why she chose to become a hip hop singer. The album included songs like 'Rolling the Dice', 'Prison Cell 226', and 'It was the situation' – and it immediately reached platinum sales. She was the second top-selling singer at Dion Records after Sky. Sabrina chose to shoot the music video of 'I am sorry' in Seshego, Hillbrow and

Alexandra, and it was a huge success with the video flying off the shelves. Sabrina was becoming famous in a short time and the media was predicting that she would be Sky's main competition. That didn't sit well with Sky.

From day one the two artists had not seen eye to eye, and Sky was no longer being given as much attention at Dion Records – the focus was now on Sabrina. Hunter did not see it that way. To him, Sabrina and Sky were colleagues, both recording for the same label, and he wanted them to work together. But it was impossible for the two starts to work together.

Sky terminated her contract in February 1999 to start her own label, called LAM Records. LAM was an abbreviation of her full names, Lucky Atlega Molapo. The studio was based in Rosebank in Johannesburg and she was the one hundred per cent shareholder. Blaza followed her to be her producer, and she asked Lenny Schoeman to be her manager, and Leeu de Jager to be studio manager. Boy Max also left Dion Records to sign on with LAM Records, but Sky was looking for new talent, not dogs who were already in the game.

Lenny had seen a boy playing country music at Queenswood Park, Riaan Holton, and convinced Sky to give him a chance. She was fine with that as she wanted new talent. Riaan was born on a farm in Lephalale, but his parents divorced when he was two months old and his mother left with him to go back to her parents' house in Queenswood in Pretoria. He was nineteen years old and trying to make a living. His plan was to make money to buy his mother a house. Riaan was always happy and laughing. Growing up without a father had taught him to be a man from an early age and to appreciate life. At LAM Records, they shortened his name to Ray, and he recorded an album called *Letter to Jessica* that sold gold soon after it was released, bringing success to Sky's new record label.

Paul 'King' Mabuza also left Dion Records and signed a deal with LAM Records. King had not been a top-selling artist at Dion Records but Sky gambled and gave him a chance – in any case, he was a home boy from Mpumalanga. King was born at Verena, about a hundred kilometres from Mak ville. King had left Verena at the age of seventeen to live with his mother in Mamelodi West after both his grandparents had passed on. Because there was no one to take care of King in Verena, they decided he would complete his high school in Mamelodi. In Mamelodi he heard that Dion Records was looking for talent, and he signed his first deal immediately after matric. King's parents were young and they understood modern lifestyle; they also noticed that their boy was not good when it came to books, but he was a good singer. They promised to support him in his music career as long as he first finished matric. With this agreement, they had no problems with King and he signed his deal with Dion Records. His first album was *Way Back*, and it was not successful, but other musicians backed him, saying the album was a hit, it just lacked marketing. His second album was *Lollipop*, it sold well but did not reach gold, but it was enough to please Hunter.

King's third album was with LAM Records, called *Bakau*, which included hit songs like 'Great Wall of China', 'Indian Girl Lalita', 'Mamelodi Coconuts', and 'Via Tsamaya Road'. The song, 'Bakau' was about the tragedy at Independence Stadium in the finale of the Cross Nations Tour, where four hundred people had lost their lives when the stadium collapsed. The song was popular all over the world and the album quickly reached platinum sales. This meant LAM Records was becoming the best record label in South Africa, after Dion Records, at number four in the ratings.

Boy Max also recorded a hit album, *Baby the Jet*, about Sky's Cessna Citation Jet, which sold platinum and meant that LAM was growing even bigger.

Dion Records was feeling the pressure after Sky left to start her own record label, and Hunter tried to persuade Sky to link Dion Records and LAM Records, but she refused. As soon as Sky saw that everything was going well at LAM Records, she took a break to focus on her business interests. She started a large poultry farm called SKY Pol, located east of Johannesburg on a farm in Nigel, which was soon exporting poultry meat to European countries, South Asia, Hawaii, and the Caribbean. When she realised the farm was not big enough to satisfy the demand, she built another farm in Standerton, which was larger than the one in Nigel.

Sky also expanded Queen Restaurants, which had only been in Sandton and Cape Town in South Africa, to Hawaii's capital, Honolulu, and then she bought a beach house in Waikiki with a private beach.

Sky also bought twenty per cent shares in a South African shipping company, Denver Shipping, that transported goods all over the world, but specialised in shipping large machinery such as generators, military tanks, air control towers, yachts, mining equipment, cars, and much else.

Sky started to boast to the media that she had money like dust, which was true as she was a multi-billionaire in 1999. The beef between her and Hunter was also worsening, to the point that the media were part of it. When they asked her why she left Dion Records because Hunter had introduced her to the music industry, she said, "Hunter didn't build me, I made him."

Sky bought a luxury yacht that she named, Group Eight, that had a bar, offices, bedrooms, sitting room, dining room, kitchens, swimming pool, a speedboat and everything needed to be a luxury yacht. She sailed from South Africa to Hawaii for a break from the music industry and to spend a month at her home in Waikiki and check on her restaurants. In her spare time, she visited towns, shopping, visiting museums, relaxing on beaches, and also looking for new business opportunities, especially in Kakaako and Chinatown. After a month, she sailed on Group Eight to Nepal in South Asia, spending two months in Kathmandu and visiting Keladighat, southwest in Nepal. When she returned to South Africa after three months, she found that the media was saying that Sabrina was the next queen of hip hop after dropping another hit song she called 'Number One', which applauded herself as number one, and indirectly criticising Sky as a sham.

> *Sabrina! I am the Hip Hop Queen, the original*
> *I am shaking the Himalayas with my rap*
> *hey! Watch out the Mountains fall*
> *I shift the Mountains with my Hip Hop sound*

I'm number
the Queen of Hip Hop
I don't fake, I'm the original
not the fake Bitches claiming to be Queens
trading some panties to get some business deals
living fake life, fake Love
She's a bitch slipping with married man
wakeup smelling another woman's colon
no man want you cause you don't have a taste
fake bitch living in the big world
cruising, mentions, living in the fast but stupid
I'm now in the industry doing my thing
you scared
you running cause you don't have to beat me in
*   this game*
is my game, I own it and I make the rules
you a cockroach
I gonna crush you with my feet
damn! I'm the original
I'm number one, bitch!

Critics said the song 'Number One' was not a hit and the album was not something they expected from Sabrina, but the album sold platinum anyway because people want to hear the lyrics. In interviews, Sabrina denied that the song was about Sky, but the lyrics were clear. Sabrina said she wrote the song in prison to deal with her anger, but when Sky heard the song, she recorded an album she called *Hillbrow Life*, responding to Sabrina's song.

From north to south, east to west they scream
        my name
they found me in the industry and left me in the
        industry
who are you?
Coming in the music yesterday and already calling
        yourself a Queen
girl, set you record straight
shut your mouth if you do not have a song
stop rapping bullshit
oh! Yeah, I have a mention in Cape Town, Hawaii,
        Waterkloof
driving a Chevy, a Bima and a Cadillac limo
chilling with the big guns discussing big deals
drinking wines import bottles from Italy, whiskies,
        tequilas, smoking cigars
I don't sleep on the sheets
I'm sleeping on the Benjamins
so what?
You claim to be a Hip Hop Queen but we all know
        you Hillbrow Queen, a jail bird
I'm living a big life and not a Hillbrow life
I hustle the dollars and you hustle the peanuts
cheap girl, selling body all night for bread and you
        call that hustling
I'm the billionaire and there nothing you can do
Hoof!

The day after *Hillbrow Life* was released, people were in music shops all over the world, buying the album. Within a week the first stock was sold out and orders were being placed for it. It was very rare in the history of the music industry for people to place orders to buy an album. This is when the media realised that Sky was fighting for her throne, and the album was classed as the best she had ever released, selling double platinum. Every song on the album was a hot coal, such as the song loved by the youth called 'Hip hop will never die.'

I love all types of music as long it has a message
    and a beat that rocks
Sky is from Afropop and country music
then I abandoned Rose the guitar
sorry I was not loyal to you
something changed my focus
listening to Hip Hop music
I loved the way they rap
looking at the music videos of Hip Hop artist
wearing expensive clothes, tattoos and white Nike
    sneakers
gold dollar chains, gold tooth, gold watch, gold
    everything
living on a fast lane, fast life
then I chose Hip Hop
Living life the way I want
cruising on a N1, fast lane
I don't care what critics say
I dropped the first album, the world was waking up
I dropped the second album and I shook the world
then I dropped the single and people couldn't believe
    I can do miracles
now I dropped another one people are crazy

Dude, I'm telling you
Hip Hop will never die
After these lyrics she spoke until the end of the song.
When I was growing up my parents 'wannet' to feed
*   me education*
they always 'wannet' me to be a teacher
well … I became a teacher as they wished but …
it was their wish not mine
my heart always lust for a microphone
singing my lungs out to the world
and I made it
I chose Hip Hop and they can feel me
I can express my feeling a speak with Hip Hop
*   music*
four pillars of the world people can hear my music
I never thought life can be so good
waking up in a twenty-eight room house
naked walking to the kitchen to open a five thousand
*   rand wine bottle*
hahaha! … Sorry for laughing I just never thought
*   life can be like that*
eating one thousand rand meals facing the ocean
even if die one day don't cry because I lived my life
*   in a fast lane*
and that is how I 'wannet'
it happened because of Hip Hop
Hip Hop will live forever and I will be the guardian
let me get out of here to relive my mind
cruise to the Bahamas to visit the Bahamians
with my million dollar luxury yacht

The song played everywhere, in taxis, restaurants, clothing shops, and on just about every radio station around the world. Even Hunter congratulated her in the media. Sky sang the album for the first time on stage at Soccer City in Soweto when she was raising funds for SKYCF to build schools for poor communities in a village called Qumbu in the Eastern Cape.

The campaign was a success and enough funds were raised to build two schools – a primary school called Lucky Molapo Primary School, and a middle school combined with a senior secondary school called Atlega Molapo High School. In the same year in 1999, Sky started a campaign to climb Mount Kilimanjaro to help people living with HIV/Aids, and she donated R350 million to The Aids Foundation, which was doing good work among people affected by the deadly virus.

On 5 December 1999, it was a beautiful sunny Sunday, and at about ten o'clock in the morning, Sky drove her white Mercedes Benz E320 to the filling station to buy the newspapers. According to eyewitnesses, as she returned home and was waiting for the gate to open, a white BMW 325 IS with dark tinted windows came around the corner at high speed and stopped behind Sky's car. Two African men jumped out with AK47s and ran to the driver's window and started shooting. When the police arrived, they found the lifeless body of hip hop star, Lucky Atlega 'Sky' Molapo inside her car with multiple gunshot wounds. There was blood everywhere inside the vehicle, and bullet holes from one side of the car to the other. Eyewitnesses identified that there were two African males who had been shooting and the vehicle they were driving, but they didn't see the BMW's number plate.

Police all over Gauteng were alerted to search for her killers, and soon the story was all over the media. Police found Sky's cell phone in the car and they dialled the number that had been dialled several times, under the name 'Sister'. When they called, the person who answered was Lebogang Monkoe. The police told her about the passing of Sky, and Lala dropped a glass of water she was fetching for Baby. Even though Lala was a neighbour, she was like a sister to Sky, and when Sky built a house for her parents, she included rooms for Lala to stay there and look after her parents when Sky was not around, as she would often be away for months at a time.

It was hard to tell Sky's parents about their daughter's violent death. Lala started crying and she slowly slid down the wall in the sitting room in disbelief. Sky's parents came rushing over to Lala to fund out what was wrong, but she couldn't talk. Eventually she caught her breath and told them the terrible news. At first they could not believe what she told them, then Sky's mother fell down in a dead faint, and her father tried to be strong, but after a few minutes he broke into tears.

The next day it headline news everywhere. In the newspapers, the headlines were, 'Motherland Queen shot at her Waterkloof home,' 'Lucky Molapo died at the age of 24' 'Who killed Sky?' 'Hip hop singer Sky dies', 'Businesswoman Lucky Atlega Molapo shot', 'Founder of LAM Records killed' and the news reached international media.

Lala drove Sky's parents to identify her at the mortuary, and indeed, it was their little baby. The autopsy revealed that Sky was shot more than twenty times, with bullets puncturing her body all over. Six bullets went through her head and thirteen punctured her lungs and heart. They went to Sky's Waterkloof home were people were standing outside mourning and placing flowers outside her gates. It was even worse when people saw Sky's parents enter the property, and the media watched that sad moment closely.

Sky's college friends contacted Lala and all came to the Waterkloof home to mourn with the Molapo family – Popla, Lee, Small, Joman, Bongani and Itumeleng. It was the first time Group Eight had reunited since college, and the sad thing was that one of the group was no more, and it felt as if her death was their fault because they had failed to look after her as they had at college.

Three weeks before, Sky had given Lala a key and told her it was the key to the safe in her Waterkloof home, and if anything happened to her, Lala was to open the safe and sit with her parents and go through the contents of the safe. Sky had not told her what was in the safe. Sky had asked Lala to promise that she would not open the safe unless something happened to her. Lala was surprised, but she agreed. Lala suspected that Sky had known that someone was trying to kill her, but had not said anything to anyone. People had accused Dion Hunter because he had beef with Sky after she left Dion Records. They also suspected Hunter because on the day she was shot, she didn't have the Dion Bouncers bodyguards with her, but the truth was that Sky preferred to be alone most of the time, unless she was on an official trip.

Some suspected Sabrina had hired hit men to eliminate Sky as competition, and some believed it was robbery, but

nothing had been taken. Some suggested her business part-
ners had killed her.

Lala was sitting in Sky's bedroom with Sky's parents
when she opened the safe. In it were a lot of pictures of
places she had travelled to, a letter, a CD labelled 'Good
Night', SKY label sneakers studded with diamonds, white
bucket jeans and a t-shirt with the words 'Death is the
Limit' printed on it, and about twenty gold necklaces that
she had worn on the closing day of the Cross Nations Tour
in Gambia.

The letter was four pages long, telling them about the
properties she had all over the world, the names of business
people she was doing business with, pin codes of her bank
cards and the attorney who would handle her estate. They
looked at the pictures with happiness realising that Sky
enjoyed her life, and they believed she would rest in peace.
After looking at the pictures, Lala played the CD on a
stereo in Sky's bedroom. It was a hip hop song.

> *If you hear this song then you know I'm gone*
> *I just 'wanna' say goodbye to all the people who*
>   *supported me*
> *you showed me love every day and I appreciate it*
> *walking down the street and asking autographs*
> *Screaming my name when I'm on stage*
> *buying my copies to support my music*
> *always asking when I'm going to drop an album*
> *always 'wanna' be where I am*
> *just to hear my Hip Hop music*
> *I really appreciate from the bottom of my heart*
> *tell my people in Mak ville I say good night*

you must not cry cause I'm sleeping not dead
(Chorus)
this is good night ... it is not goodbye
bury me at dawn before sunrise
engrave my coffin with the words of love
take me down with the Hip Hop songs (2x)
They say God also wants the good ones
I hope He will let me to sing Hip Hop music in
    Heaven
I never thought the day would come
but it's ok cause I lived my life like it is the last day
I cruised, from South Africa to Hawaii
from Hawaii to the Bahamas
and from Bahamas to Nepal
eating with knife and fork
learning to eat with chopsticks
all the days I spent in studio
performing, travelling nine province of South Africa
Africa, Europe, Asia, Russia, America, everywhere
climbing the mountain of Kilimanjaro
thanks to my mother and my father they raised
    me well
thanks to my sister that cared about me
all of my friends in college that protected me
I am the Hip Hop Queen and did hold my throne
Life is a novel book with bad ending story
you won't see me again but my name will remain
you must not cry cause I'm sleeping not dead
(Chorus)
This is good night ... it is not good bye
bury me at dawn before sunrise

engrave my coffin with the words of love
take me down with the Hip Hop songs (2x)

Rachel Myburgh was Sky's personal assistant who helped Sky run the companies when Sky was taking a break. She knew every details about Sky's empire, according to the letter. Sky's parents had never met Rachel, but Lala had met her couple of time, which was not surprising as Sky shared most of things with Lala. Rachel volunteered to organise the funeral. She drove Sky's parents and Lala to choose a coffin, and they found a craftsman to engrave messages of love all over it. They asked her friends to write love messages to put on the coffin.

The family together with Lala chose a luxurious coffin that was gold in colour, engraved with messages of love, and large black and bold words that said, 'Death is my Limit'.

Pretoria was packed with people attending her memorial service that was held at Pretoria Hall on 9 December. VIPs from all over the world attended, as did Hunter and Dion Records artists. Several African presidents sent message of condolence to the Molapo family.

People criticised Hunter's attendance as he was a suspect in the police investigations, but Lala, as the family's representative, told the media that everyone was welcome to attend Sky's funeral because no one is guilty until proven guilty.

On 10 December 1999, the body of Sky was transported from her Waterkloof home to Mak ville' where she would be buried the following day, which was a Saturday.

Outside the Waterkloof home, neighbours and thousands of people gathered to say goodbye to Sky for the last time. People could see the coffin inside through the hearse windows, and they could not hold back their tears when it drove out of Sky's home. Police vehicles escorted the vehicle together with a motorcade that was about two kilometres long, with sirens wailing to open the road to pass.

People lined the streets of the city and the villages the funeral procession passed through to pay their respects and honour the Hip Hop Queen. In Mak ville, it was the same, as it had been on the day Sky and her friends had first left to go to Kwandebele College, and the day she came home after releasing her first album.

People in the motorcade were emotional when they saw the community of Mak ville and neighbouring areas wearing white t-shirts printed with, 'Death is the Limit.'

On 11 December 1999, Sky was laid to rest in Mak ville cemetery at six o'clock in the morning. As the coffin was lowered, they read the obituary and played the song, 'Be Happy Mama'. The cloud that was hanging over the cemetery brought down light showers, and then a rainbow adorned the sky. The community of Mak ville believes it only rains when you bury a king, chief, queen, prince or princess, and the people in and around the cemetery looked up with smiles.

The truth was Sefako had run away from his kingship throne to seek refuge in Mak ville after some of his family members had attempted to eliminate him a couple of times. It was only the Chief of Mak ville who knew the Molapo family secrets. The rumours were that Sefako was brought by his father to the Chief of Mak ville for protection. The Chief built Sefako a house, and after a few months, Baby came to stay with him as his wife. No one questioned Sefako and Baby's roots.

After the funeral, an attorney named Brenda Memela approached the Molapo family. Sefako asked Lala to stay close as she was involved in the Molapo's family matters. The woman told them she was the attorney who was going to handle Sky's estate and she asked the family for a date to discuss the estate.

Brenda Memela opened a document to read the names of people who needed to be present – Popi Skosana, Lerato Ranaka, Lebogang Monkoe, Jovan Makola, Collen Masango, Itumeleng Given Manaka, and Bongani Mahlangu. The Molapos were not surprised because they had met those people who Lala introduced as their college friends.

A date was set for the following week to meet at Sky's house in Waterkloof and on the day, everyone gathered to hear the detail of the estate.

Group Eight could not believe that Sky had included them in her estate and knowing that she was a billionaire, they were certain the cut was going to be big. They were right. Sky gave them twenty-five per cent of the money to share, and the remaining seventy-five per cent was for her parents. In the will she had written a letter, "If you listening to this message then you know I am dead ok. My parents, you deserve this money, and friends, I give you a share because you gave me support and love at college. Even if you were not around after college, I was ok because you played your part and this is how I say thank you. I will always love you guys."

The will allocated all her property to be managed under SKYCF, excluding the houses in Waterkloof, Cape Town, and Hawaii, which she gave to her parents, and if her parents passed away, they would go to her parents' guardian, Lebogang Monkoe. Sky wanted Lebogang Monkoe to be the permanent General Manager of SKYCF, and Rachel Myburgh to be the Financial Officer. Every company she owned, every share she had, Baby the Jet, the Group Eight Yacht, and LAM Records must all be the property of SKYCF under Lebogang Monkoe's management.

According to the will, no one had the right to sell the property – it would be the property of her parents, Lebogang Monkoe, and the children of the guardian, and generations to come, as she didn't have children or siblings.

The will mentioned that her parents were entitled to twenty per cent of the profit from every company, and had the wight to request an annual report from SKYCF. The diamond shoes that she was wearing at the closing of the Cross Nations Tour could be sold at a price determined by her parents.

That was the end of the will.

In early 2000 the diamond shoes were sold to the museum of Pretoria for millions of rand and LAM Records erected a statue of Lucky Atlega 'Sky' Molapo at the entrance of the village of Makometsane as a memorial.

The local government built a park at Mak ville named the Lucky Molapo Park and a hall that was named Sky Hall in loving memory of their Hip Hop Queen.

Vincent Mo'Russia changed the name of Mzala to Sky ville, and hung pictures of Sky playing onstage, showing

Mzala before the renovations, with the permission of her parents.

LAM Records released an album she had recorded, which included the song found in the safe in the Waterkloof home called 'Good Night'. The title of the album was a song Sky had recorded a week before she was shot, called 'Thinking'.

Sometimes when I'm alone and the boredom strike
I sit at the back and look in the pool
I open the wine then put the whisky closer
light the cigar and think
where is Heaven or is there a map?
Do we drive there or just walk?
Take a boat or just swim?
Fly there or just show up in Heaven as soon as we
*   lose breath*
Do we need a ticket to enter or just walk in?
Is it a safe place or are there greedy people like on
*   earth?*
If I go there now, will I be safe?
Is Heaven a Continent, Country or a region?
Maybe is a City, Town or Suburb
if Jesus says we can all fit then it must be an
*   endless world*
maybe,
I wonder if God will let me sing
will he let me continue to keep Hip Hop alive
I wish He can appoint me to be an angel of
*   Hip Hop*
the guardian of Hip Hop if Heaven exists

asking myself so many questions without answers
stupid questions
even if I ask people no one will have an answer
why bother
let me wait for the day because is where everyone is
    going
they say

The album included love songs like 'Handsome', a collaboration of different artist singing a song called 'Til we meet again', a song by King called 'Who killed Sky?' and it won the award for best hip hop album of the year in 2000.

In early 2001, the Molapo family applied for citizenship in Hawaii, which was granted after a few months, and later that year the community of Mak ville said goodbye to the family.

Lala went with the family to respect her friend's wish of being their guardian, but in any event, they had always treated Lala like their second daughter.

The Molapo family had struggled to heal after the passing of their daughter and moving to Waikiki was a way of healing. It was after all, the place where Sky had gone to regain her strength.

Eight years after the passing of Sky, Group Eight went to Mak ville cemetery to visit her grave, and they couldn't hold back their tears. The grave had the biggest tombstone in the cemetery. It had a guitar on top and it was engraved, 'REST IN PEACE, LUCKY ATLEGA MOLAPO, QUEEN OF HIP POP' in big bold letters that could be seen from far.

They stood around the grave, talking about their days in college as if Sky was present, but tears were falling, mixed with their smiles. After grieving, they cleaned the tombstone and the grass that surrounded the grave, and it became a yearly thing to visit her grave.

The murder of Motherland Queen is still a cold case; no one was arrested because there was no evidence, and the questions remains, "Who killed Lucky Atlega 'Sky' Molapo?"

ABOUT THE AUTHOR

Aggrey Mokone: is working in the South African Police Services as Chief Admin Clerk. Studied at University of South Africa and obtained a Qualification in Refugee Law and Humanitarian support NQF level 5 and Creative writing NQF level 5. "Death is the limit" is my first project, a Novella fiction book. Inspired by the way I think about life, most of the time I sit alone and built stories of inspiration but realises is better to write them in books to share my thoughts with the world. My vision is to see books that I wrote interpreted to short films locally and internationally.

www.ingramcontent.com/pod-product-compliance
Lightning Source LLC
Chambersburg PA
CBHW030306130626
46549CB00002B/724